Lost in You

SWANSON COURT SERIES

Book Three

SERENA GREY

ISBN-10: 1519145411
ISBN-13: 978-1519145413

Dedication

To all the awesome authors who wrote the stories that made me dream of writing mine.

And to my readers, always.

Acknowledgements

My Beta-readers –Terri Thomas, Ashley Ambrose, Mary Hanft, Debbie Duncalf, my ARC reviewers, readers, supporters, cheerleaders, friends, family, husband… all those people who make me want to laugh and smile and cry at the same time because of how wonderful you are.

Thank you.

Lost in You

One night.
One love.
One heart.
One forever.

The concluding part of the Swanson Court Trilogy

What do you do when you take a leap of faith, and you don't get what you expected?

You move on.

That is exactly what Rachel plans to do, to put aside her heartbreak, and concentrate on her work and the people she loves.

But Landon is not easy to forget. When he reappears in her life, is he offering the perfect ending she wants more than anything, or just another flirtation with heartbreak, pain, danger, and devastating loss.

1

I love fall in New York. The crisp air, brilliant colors, clear skies, and beautiful sunsets. But today, as the car from the airport comes to a stop outside my building, I hardly notice those things.

Once again, I've walked away from the man I love, even though it was the last thing I wanted to do. I still feel a strange kind of certainty from baring my feelings to Landon, but I can't help wishing that things had turned out differently.

But they hadn't. Landon reacted to my confession that I was in love with him, not with pity and regret, as I'd feared, or reciprocation as I'd hoped, but with the fear that somehow, he was going to hurt me.

That meant something, at least. It meant that I could hope. That maybe, just maybe, he could conquer whatever fears from his past made him reluctant to commit to me, the way I was committed to him.

Now I only have to wait. Sometimes, holding on is not the answer. Sometimes, you have to let go and let love find a way to work. If Landon's feelings for me are strong enough for him to want to build something with me, he knows where to find me. If he chooses to let me go, then I'll have no excuse to keep dwelling on him. I'll have no choice but to move on.

And I'm strong enough to do that.

With that thought, I start to fish for the keys to my apartment inside my purse. The Swanson Court driver who picked me up at the airport is still standing at the top of the stairs, carrying my luggage. "Thank you," I tell him with a small smile. "You can leave it here."

He does as I say, giving me a polite nod before leaving. I let myself into the apartment, pausing at the door when I see Laurie and Brett on the couch. They're facing each other, their heads close together and their hands clasped.

When they notice me, Brett starts to get up, still holding Laurie's hands. His eyes are glistening with tears, contrasting with the wide heartfelt smile on his face.

I turn a puzzled glance to Laurie, who's also standing now, facing me. She has definitely been crying, her cheeks are wet, but like Brett, she's smiling through the tears.

"Hi Rachel," she says softly.

Her voice tells me that it's okay to hope that something has gone right. I look from her face to Brett's, then back again. "Please tell me you're not fighting anymore," I whisper.

Laurie shakes her head. She lets out a happy laugh. "No, we're not."

Taking the few steps to where she's standing, I envelop her in a hug before turning to Brett. "Glad to see you finally got it together," I tell him, hugging him too.

"Me too, Rach." He returns my hug and kisses both my cheeks. His eyes are still glistening. "Thank you," he whispers.

"I'm just so happy for you both." I roll my eyes at Laurie. "Finally!"

"We're going to get married," she tells me, an edge of excitement in her voice. She releases a shaky breath, as if she doesn't quite believe it yet. "We're getting married," she repeats.

I turn to Brett, my eyes wide and my mouth open. He nods in confirmation and I scream, throwing my arms around Laurie again. "Oh Laurie! I'm so happy." Now, I'm actually crying with happiness. "Wow!" I give her an arch look, "A lot happened while I was gone."

Laurie giggles, "You wouldn't believe."

"I have to get back to the gym," Brett says. He's still grinning, his chest swelled with happiness. He bends to kiss Laurie on the forehead and she leans into him, wrapping her arms around his waist. Their intimacy and emotional connection is palpable, and I might as well not even be in the room.

After a few seconds, they reluctantly pull apart. "I'll leave you two to catch up," Brett continues, his hand lingering around Laurie's. He finally lets it drop so he can give me another quick hug. "I'll come back later," he tells Laurie, before leaving.

I wait for the door to close behind him then I scream again and give Laurie another excited hug. "How did this happen?"

She sighs happily and falls back on the couch. "Where do I begin?"

"At the beginning!" I throw up my hands. "Last night, you said… you and Chadwick…" I join her on the couch. "What the fuck happened?"

She covers her face, giggling behind her hands. "I couldn't do it." She drops her hands and gives me a shamefaced look before shaking her head. "I just couldn't. I went there thinking that maybe I needed to get under someone else so I could get over Brett, and I was ready to. Chadwick is cute and sexy, you know?"

"Yeah…?" I shrug. "So what happened?"

"We got talking. Me and Chadwick. The food was horrible, God!" She grimaces. "Anyway, we drank wine, got slightly drunk, then I started talking about Brett, and even though I knew somewhere in my head that this was a date and I was supposed to be thinking about doing the dirty with Chadwick, I just couldn't stop talking about Brett."

"Poor Chadwick." I sigh. "How did he react?"

"He listened." Laurie smiles. "He's really sweet, isn't he? Underneath all that, *'I can't wait to get into your pants'* swagger."

I laugh at her description of Chadwick's harmless flirting. "He is," I agree.

"Anyway," Laurie continues, "At some point, it just became clear that what I needed wasn't some quick fix to try to get over Brett. What I really needed was to tell him how I felt, to listen to him and try to make it work."

I hug myself. "Awww. That's so sweet."

Laurie swats me playfully. "Chadwick called me a cab, and on the way, I called Brett. I took my own advice and told him everything I was feeling, my fears, everything I thought he didn't understand." She smiles. "He came over, we fought, made up, cried… Then it just kinda slipped out that he wanted us to spend the rest of our lives together. He didn't plan to." She holds up her hand. "See, no ring."

I blink back tears. "I'm just glad you're happy."

"Me too." Her eyes start to glisten and she blinks rapidly. "I can hardly believe how happy I am. I can't believe I was going to throw it all away because of a stupid hug in front of a stupid diner." She looks at me. "He explained all about that too. She left her boyfriend and moved here to escape the 'small town life' and she's been incredibly lonely, struggling with the desire to move back home, trying to find reasons to stay, but she's finally leaving, and the diner was her goodbye lunch. Brett wasn't even the only one there from the gym. He just came out with her because he was leaving too. Everyone else was still inside."

"Really?" I chuckle, "And you made me power walk almost the whole way home."

"Sorry." She gives me a sheepish look. "I feel sorry now that I didn't listen to him, but maybe we needed to go through all that to get here."

I sigh. "You're right," I agree softly.

She takes my hand. "How did it go with Landon?"

I told him how I felt.

But he couldn't bring himself to say he feels the same way.

Because maybe he doesn't.

"I…" I shrug. "I don't really want to talk about it, not right now."

Laurie gives me a long look, and for a moment, I think she's going to insist. I really don't want to talk about Landon. It's not just because it would hurt me to remember, but also because I don't want to tell her how last night went and be the one ruin the happiness of the moment.

Thankfully, Laurie changes the subject and starts to tell me more about what she and Brett talked about through the night. She's full of excitement and happiness, but she hasn't slept all night, so it's not long before she's nodding off.

After Laurie goes off to bed, I prepare for a nap too, wondering what Landon's reaction was when he woke up in the morning and found that I had left him yet again. When I'd called Tony Gillies to arrange for my return on one of the early flights back to New York, I'd been afraid that he'd try to clear it with his boss, and some hopeful part of me had expected Landon to do something, like try to stop me.

But he hadn't.

I'd flown back with Aidan, and even though we had a lively conversation on the plane, for some reason, we didn't talk about Landon. It was almost as if he understood that there was something wrong, and that I would break apart at the mention of his brother's name. In New York, a Swanson Court International town car had been waiting to drive me home. During the drive to my apartment, I waited for my phone to ring, for Landon to call, to tell me something, anything to make me believe that something good would come out of what I'd told him last night.

But there was nothing.

When I'm under the covers, my arms curled around a pillow, I allow myself to think of the way Landon held me after I told him I loved him, the way his body shook, the tenderness with which he made love to me, and the tears start to fall.

I have to face the fact that we may never end up like Laurie and Brett, because not every love story has a happy ending. Maybe his aversion to commitment will overshadow his feelings for me. Maybe he'll choose to continue the way he always has, and find someone else who would be willing to accept his terms of a commitment-free relationship, someone who wouldn't make him face emotions he'd rather not feel.

Maybe he'll forget about me.

Almost choking on the thought, I swallow my sobs and force myself to think of other happier things. I close my eyes, willing myself to fall asleep, and to believe that no matter what happens, I'll be able to handle it.

Days pass, and my strength starts to falter. I don't hear from Landon, and the longer his silence lasts, the more an empty numbness spreads inside me. Every day, Rafael picks me up from my apartment for the drive to the Gilt building, and in the evening, he's there to pick me up again. I don't ask him about his boss, and he doesn't volunteer any information.

After a few days, Joe replaces him as my driver, a sure sign that Landon is back in town. The thought that he's staying away from me even though he's so close is almost too painful to bear. But I continue to wait, trying to be strong, trying to convince myself that whether he comes to me or not, I can live with it.

He doesn't come, but from all directions, I'm

assailed with news about him. The media is ecstatic about the Gold Dust, and the reviews are beyond marvelous. He even makes the cover of a popular news daily. **"Glitz And Glamour as Landon Court Opens New Hotel,"** the headline screams, with a heartbreakingly beautiful picture of Landon on the cover.

I can't resist reading that, as well as the numerous articles on the internet. Many of them dwell on the connection with Ava, whose family originally owned the hotel, and they pair their articles with pictures of Landon with her. Only a few of them mention me as Landon Court's date. But why should they bother? I'm just one in the long list of *'dates'* that had come and gone.

I read about Landon's trip to Europe as the guest of the head of a corporate group with interests in hotels worldwide. There's a party on a large boat, with lots of models and actresses. In the pictures, I can tell nothing from Landon's face. As always, he maintains his detachment, his seeming lack of interest in the things going on around him, and looking at his face, I wonder if he's thinking about me at all.

His successes continue - rumors of the acquisition of a Vegas property, a news publication publishing a retraction and apology about a negative article written about him. Investors courting him…

Five days.

Without a word.

And just like that, the sliver of hope I'd been holding on to, disappears, along with the belief that what he felt for me, the things I'd felt in his arms, would conquer whatever held him back. I have to face the knowledge that when I walked away from his suite in San Francisco, I had finally and irrevocably ended us.

Everyone around me is ecstatic about Laurie and Brett. I am too, but in my current state of mind, I'm not strong enough to be constantly cheerful and excited. The effort it takes to hide my pain is draining, but I have to, for Laurie.

"Your auntie Jacie thinks we should go to Barbados for the wedding. I think it's an excellent idea. A change of scene for all of us. What do you think?"

I'm on the phone with my mother, and we're having yet another conversation about the wedding. Our parents are over the moon, of course, and my mom and aunt Jacie have made and shelved enough plans in one short week than most wedding planners make in a year.

"I would love to go to Barbados," I tell her. If anybody needs a change of scene, it's probably me. Laurie's grandmother, Auntie Jacie's mom, lives in Bridgetown, and over the years, we've spent a few holidays in the Barbadian city. Having the wedding over there meant that Nana wouldn't have to travel, and Laurie could have her wedding in one of the most beautiful beaches in the world.

"It would be lovely wouldn't it? Taylor and Jacie will iron it all out with Brett's parents, and we'll make a holiday out of it."

"Is that what Laurie wants?" I ask, knowing that my mom and Aunt Jacie could very well make a plan and run halfway with it before checking with Laurie. It was just their nature.

"Yeah…" she says slowly. "I believe Jacie's talked about it with her."

I chuckle. "If Laurie's okay with it, I don't see why not."

"Exactly!" I can tell my mom is excited at the thought. She starts to go on about plans, color schemes, flowers and so on while I do my best to pay attention.

"Laurie told me that you and Landon have run into another hiccup," she says finally, when she's out of other things to say.

A hiccup? I sigh. Talk about making a molehill out of a mountain. "I don't really want to talk about it mom."

"Okay," she says quickly. "But if or when you do, I'm here, all right?"

"Got it."

We're both silent. "Are we going ahead with the engagement party?" I ask, changing the subject.

It works. "Of course!" she exclaims. "We're thinking next weekend, but we'll conclude tomorrow at dinner with Brett's parents. We're looking forward to seeing you."

Laurie's dad is taking us all to dinner at his old club. The three sets of parents, Laurie, Brett and me. Another evening of trying to be cheerful and happy, when deep inside, I just want to curl up somewhere and cry. "I can't wait," I say brightly.

"Good." She sighs. "Your father says hi."

"Hi dad," I call out.

I hear his voice in the background followed by my mom's laughter. "See you tomorrow sweetheart," she says, "and take care of yourself," she adds softly.

On Saturday evening, I join my family at the private club where we're all having dinner, apart from Dylan, who's in school. Brett arrives with Laurie, and his parent's join us a few minutes later. Hugs and kisses are exchanged all around, and dinner is served at the large table we reserved while the parents bond, talking wedding plans, retirement, and then wedding plans again.

After dinner, Brett and Laurie get up to dance to a slow song the band is playing. I watch them from the table, happy for them, and yet, envious of their happiness.

"You look like you need a break," my mom remarks, leaning toward me. Her remarkably youthful face is only marred by her expression of concern. "Have you been working too hard? You should come home and rest a little."

I shake my head, wondering how much of my misery is evident on my face. "I'm fine, mom."

"No, you're not," she whispers. "I'm your mother, and I have eyes. I can see that you're not *fine*."

I paste a bright, fake smile on my face and give her a pointed look. "Do I look miserable? Mom, I'm perfectly happy."

She looks at my dad for help, a sign that they've shared their concern about me. I take a frustrated breath and close my eyes, hating the fact that they're worried enough about me for it to be an issue they've discussed.

My dad gets up and comes over to take my hand. "Come on," he says. "Humor your old man with a dance."

"Your mother's just worried about you," he tells me, when we join Laurie and Brett on the floor.

"I know," I reply. "I'm not mad. It's just… I'm fine, really."

He nods, buying the lie, or at least pretending to. "Well then, let's give your cousin and her fiancé a run for their money." He signals to the band and they change the music to a livelier number, and somehow, for the rest of the evening, I'm able to let go of my pain and actually enjoy myself.

The final consensus is that there's going to be an engagement party on the coming weekend. We're home on Sunday evening when Laurie receives the news while on the phone with her mother.

"What does an engagement party even mean?" She grumbles, pretending to be pissed, though I can clearly see that she's enjoying all the attention. We're eating chips from a bag, passing it back and forth while we watch a bunch of hot-ish guys talk about how excited they all are to be vying for one 'lucky' woman's love.

"Usually it means parents want any excuse for a party," I tell her, laughing. "But this time, it makes sense to have one. There's bound to be a couple of people who won't be able to make it to Barbados for the wedding."

Laurie makes a face, then spends a long moment admiring the stunning yellow diamond on her finger. Brett had quickly remedied the absence of a ring during his proposal, and Laurie was in love with the spectacular ring he'd bought her. "Do you think it's silly, going all the way to Barbados to get married when we could just go to Vegas and get done with it?"

"Of course not! Your Nana would never forgive you if you pulled a Vegas stunt. Neither would your mom or mine for that matter." I shake my head, imagining the catastrophe that would result if she did something like that. "At least, nobody's asking you to be part of the preparations for the engagement party. They're probably having a swell time planning it."

"I know." She sighs and reaches for the bag of chips. I hand it to her, my eyes going back to the TV. One of the guys is earnestly telling the camera why he thinks he's the right one for the woman in question. I roll my eyes at the ridiculousness.

"He still hasn't called at all?" Laurie's voice is soft.

I shake my head without looking at her. It's been a week and one day now. "I don't think…" I pause, willing myself to say the words without falling to pieces. "I don't think he's going to call again."

Laurie is quiet. "I'm so sorry," she says finally. "I thought… I really thought that if you told him how you felt…"

Frowning, I turn to face her. "It's not your fault. You were exactly right. I had to tell him and I'm glad I did. Imagine if I hadn't. I'd still be hanging on to him, losing a bit of myself every day. If I'd left him without letting him know that I was in love with him, then I'd be torturing myself with the questions, possibilities, and regrets, wondering if telling him would have made a difference." I shrug. "Now I know for sure that the only way he wants me is if there's no deep commitment."

"It's his loss," Laurie declares, her voice defiant. "I was convinced that he had enough sense to have fallen in love with you, but if he can't see what you're worth then he doesn't deserve you. You are beautiful, clever, funny, and all-round awesome. Landon Court has no idea what he's lost."

I only smile in reply. I'm grateful for her support, but somehow, it's much better when I don't talk about

Landon at all. I think about him. I miss him. Sometimes, I allow myself to remember how it felt to be happy, in those blissful moments when I was actually happy with him. I will always have those moments to draw on, those memories to treasure, and there's some sort of consolation that comes from that.

I finally tell Joe that I don't need him anymore. At first, he looks as if he's going to argue and he actually follows me all the way to work, driving slowly beside me. He also does it on the way back home, and the next day too, but I ignore him.

And I do my best to stop thinking about Landon.

I see him everywhere I go. Sometimes, I feel as though he's only just a few feet away, on the other side of a crowd on the street. Every car that passes seems to be one of his. Every hazy face behind the tinted windows appears to be his face. I can't seem to stop conjuring him into my consciousness.

But I have to, because I can't continue to view my separation from Landon as temporary, and the sensible thing to do is to wean myself off everything that has to do with him.

I work feverishly, researching, writing, and editing articles with Mark, who welcomes my hectic pace and doesn't hesitate to increase my workload.

Every day, I work until I'm exhausted, with barely enough energy to talk with Laurie when I get home. Luckily, she's spending most of her time with Brett, so I don't have to pretend all the time that I'm not fighting the huge block of unhappiness weighing me down.

Every day ends the same, with me trying to sleep, while my lack of Landon tortures me in my dreams. Every song takes on a new meaning and even my favorite books lose their appeal. I wake up every morning with tears on my cheeks and an ache in my heart, and even though I tell myself that it's getting better, that I'm getting better, it takes all my strength to push myself out of bed and go on with my life.

One morning, Joe isn't waiting for me downstairs. The absence of the car on the street outside my building is like the final note in the sad song of my relationship with Landon. Proof that as far as he's concerned, we're really over.

For a long moment, I stand at the door of my building, looking out at the empty street, a shaft of pain lancing through my heart. I want to go back upstairs, curl up in my bed and cry until there are no tears left, but somehow, I command my body to move, to take the steps to the sidewalk, and then to work.

It's all right, I tell myself over and over. Even if Landon doesn't want to have a place in my life, he'll always have a place in my heart. And that's alright.

2

Everything blurs into work and sleep, and the temptation to call Landon. I want to tell him that I understand why he'd want to end things, but that I would have appreciated it if he'd chosen to tell me to my face. Then I remember the way I left him in San Francisco while he was asleep. I'd been so sure that it was the right thing to do. It made sense at the time to give him the space to decide for himself that he wanted to be with me, above anything else.

Now, I'm no longer sure of anything. Just like the song, I'd left my heart in San Francisco, and it had come back to me, bloody and broken.

One day, the pain will dull. It's what I tell myself,

with more hope than any kind of certainty.

My mom has been calling almost every day to ask how I am and chatter about party plans. I suspect she's actually calling to make sure I'm all right, but I don't mind. The distraction helps. Most times, I check my emails while we talk, and today in particular, she's going on about some artist friend of hers who might be at Laurie's engagement party, when I open and read a strange email from The Gilt Review.

At first, I think it might be information about my subscription to the magazine, and I have to bite back my shock when I see that it's a response to my application, from two years ago. I frown at the screen, unsure if the invitation to schedule an interview is a mistake.

"Are you there, sweetheart?" I hear my mom say.

"Yeah…" I'm still frowning. "Something came up mom, I'll call you back."

When she's off the phone, I read the email again, unsure what to think. It's from someone called Liz Buckley, one of the senior editors over at Review. Certain that there's been some kind of mistake, I call her office, and she confirms that they want me to come in for an interview.

It's always been my dream to work at the Gilt

Review, and I'd continued to nurse that dream after I applied there, but got the job at Gilt Traveler instead. I always assumed that one day, when I made editor, I would apply again, but I never expected them to invite me for an interview two years later, without any effort on my part. I can almost swear that something like this has never happened before.

Yet, I don't want to look a gift horse in the mouth, especially with everything else that's going on in my life. I need a change of environment. I need the feeling of starting afresh, even if it's only on a different floor. By the time I leave for home at the end of the day, I'm already looking forward to my interview, hoping that I'll get the job, and that the new set of challenges and responsibilities will help me to stop dwelling on Landon Court.

The next day, I run into Jack Weyland in the ground floor lobby on my way out to lunch. I haven't seen him since the night he kissed me outside Landon's club, but I'm still pissed at him. So when I see him across the wide marble space staring at me, I look away and keep walking.

He catches up with me outside the building and falls into step beside me. "Hello, Rachel."

"Hi Jack," I say dryly, letting my voice communicate how much I don't want to talk to him.

"Come on." He stretches his hand out to stop me. "Rachel, can I just have a minute?"

Without stopping, I pull my arm out of his reach. "Don't touch me."

He swallows and steps back. "I'm sorry."

I sigh, sorry for snapping at him, but convinced that he deserved it. Slowing down, I turn to face him. "What do you want, Jack?"

"To apologize about the other night." He looks contrite. "I really am sorry."

I pause for a moment before giving him a small nod. "Okay. Can I go have my lunch now?"

"Can we at least talk?"

"No," I exclaim with a grimace, turning on my heel and starting to walk again.

He follows me. "Please," I hear him say. "Let me join you. I just want to apologize."

I don't reply, but I don't tell him to get lost either, so he follows me all the way to the deli around the corner from the office. We used to eat there together all the time, in those days when I was still waiting for him to realize that he loved me.

Now I guess he had, but it was too late, for both of us.

We make our orders, and while we're waiting for the food to arrive, I give him an impatient glare from across the table.

"I don't know why you need to make a big ceremony out of apologizing," I say. "Seriously."

Jack is quiet. "I meant what I said that night," he starts, "about my feelings for you."

I roll my eyes. "Not again, Jack. I can't do this again."

He holds up a hand. "I know. I just wanted you to know that I didn't say those things because I was jealous of Court, or the fact that you were happy. I meant them." He closes his eyes and gives me a small, sad smile. "I'm leaving Gilt."

"Oh!" I can't hide my shock. He's been at Gilt Traveler for far longer than I have. He is one of our most talented and well-traveled writers, and he actually knew how to write. I frown, not sure that I understand. "Why?"

He shrugs. "I need a change of scene, I guess."

Did that have anything to do with me? It's strange to

think that his feelings for me could be so intense that he couldn't stand to work in the same building. What an irony that would be, I think uncomprehendingly, before dismissing the idea. There was bound to be another reason.

"Where will you go?"

"I have a deal to extend my three episode specials to ten episodes seasons. So I'm moving to LA. I'll be working more closely with the producers anyway. I might as well take the distance out of the equation."

"Of course." His TV appearances had been remarkably successful. I imagine all the dangerous things he'll have to do, year after year. All the places he'd have to travel to keep people interested in watching him on TV, but that was what he loved doing, so I guess it wasn't such a bad deal.

"I'm thinking of writing a book too," Jack continues. "I've had enough experience to write a few, I think."

I nod. "You're a great writer. I'd read anything you wrote."

There is a small pause. "It's really nice to hear that," he says.

Our food arrives, and while we eat, we talk about what his life will be like in LA. There's an undercurrent of sadness in our conversation, but I choose not to dwell on it, concentrating instead on how change really was the only constant thing.

"I got an email today," I mention, deciding to tell him about my invitation from the Gilt Review. "I have an interview with the Review. The strange thing is I didn't reapply. Somehow, they responded to my application from two years ago."

Jack raises an eyebrow, then chuckles. "I guess my mom really liked you."

His mom? I remember that strange evening with Gertrude Weyland that ended with Jack trying to kiss me on the street. "What do you mean?"

"She's been in talks to take over as the new editor of Review. She finally said yes, last week, I think. She's been reviewing files from home. Maybe after talking to you she decided that she wanted to work with you."

I shake my head. I'd thought his mother had a certain charm despite the weird relationship with her son. However, what would it be like to actually work for her? And was I sure I wanted to find out?

"Is that why you're leaving Gilt?" I ask Jack. "You don't want to work in the same building as your mother?"

He shrugs noncommittally. "Maybe." After a pause, he continues. "So will you take the job if you get it?"

I think about it. "Most likely, though I don't understand at all." I give him a look. "Should I be worried?"

"Jessica Layner won't want to let you go, but if she does, my mother would be a fool not to do everything to make sure you stay with her. You're an asset at Traveler. You'll be invaluable to Review and she'd be lucky to have you."

I smile, touched by his encouragement. "Thanks."

His eyes linger on my face for a long moment. I'm done with my food, and I know that it's time to go back, to walk away, not just from the restaurant, but from Jack.

"I hope it works out in LA," I tell him.

"Yes," he grins, then sobers and reaches across the table for my hand. "I hope you'll be happy," he says. "You deserve it, and if Court gives you that, then I wish you all the best."

I look down at his hand over mine on the table, tempted to tell him that Landon and I are no longer together. I'm feeling emotional, from saying goodbye to Jack, and from the reminder about Landon and his long, painful silence.

"Thanks," I smile at Jack again, sure that my eyes are glistening. I pull my hand back from his and get up. "Thank you, Jack." I put some money on the table before I go, leaving him sitting there, sure, but not necessarily regretful, that we will never have another intimate conversation ever again.

"I'm going to move in with Brett," Laurie tells me on Thursday evening. She looks worried, unsure of how I'll react. "He asked and I said yes."

It's day twelve after Landon, and while I'm still feeling tender, I've been trying to concentrate on all the things I can still look forward to and anticipate with pleasure. My interview, for example, as well as Laurie's engagement party, and the wedding.

"When did this happen?" I ask, delighted for her.

"Today at lunch." She smiles, "You know the gym has been growing."

"Yes." They'd recently opened two more locations, and with his business partner, Brett had developed a line of fitness products and videos that had been getting rave reviews.

"Well, with the success of the gym, the bigger apartment, and us getting married, he thinks it's time."

I nod, already missing her. "It's what you want too, right?"

"Yes."

"I'm glad then." I smile at her, then cast one look around the living room of our apartment, the home we've shared for two years. "Everything's changing," I say with a sad smile. "I'm happy, but it's scary."

Laurie nods, agreeing with me. "I'll miss living with you."

"Me too."

"Will you be alright?"

I shrug. "I've been planning to kick you out forever so I don't have to watch those awful reality shows."

"You love them," she says with a playful grin. "You'll watch them when I'm gone."

"Only when I miss you."

"Probably all the time."

Suddenly we're both crying, happy and sad at the same time.

"Being grown up is so weird," Laurie says finally. "Everything was so much easier when we were kids."

Later in bed, I'm thinking of all the ways my life is going to change, when I get an alert on my phone. It's one of the email notifications I set up for news about Landon. I'm tempted to open it, to read about what he's up to, to feast my eyes on the pictures of him and wonder what he's thinking, and if he thinks about me at all.

I resist the temptation, and before I go to sleep, I delete all the alerts and notifications I set up for him. I won't be reading about him anymore. I won't continue to torture myself by dwelling on him. There's simply no need.

On Saturday, Laurie and I go upstate. The cab drops me off at my parents', before taking her the further twenty minutes to her parent's home, where the engagement party is holding. I'm spending the night at home, and then we're all going together to Uncle Taylor's and Aunt Jacie's in the morning.

My dad stays in his study most of the day, and my mom is on the phone with Aunt Jacie, and with vendors, making last minute preparations. I remain in my old room until my brother Dylan arrives, and we stay up most of the night watching movies and snacking.

In the morning, we all troop over to join Laurie and her parents. My mom immediately throws herself into bullying the decorators, the florist, and all the other vendors with Aunt Jacie, while Laurie and I watch them from upstairs. My dad and uncle have disappeared somewhere, the study or the den, and Dylan is watching TV downstairs, so it's just Laurie and me.

"It feels as if you're getting married today," I tell her.

"Right?" She sighs. "It feels as if my mom has been waiting for this moment since I was born. I don't even want to think about the real wedding."

"It'll be beautiful," I assure her.

"I know." She laughs. "I just wish all the preparations were over and we were like, married already." She looks at me. "I shouldn't be complaining though. When's your interview?"

"Next week." I sigh. "At least there's that for me to look forward to."

Laurie rises from the bed and takes my hand. "Let's have fun today. It's a party after all."

She's right. The party starts in the afternoon, spilling

from the garden into the lawn, and it is fun. After the toasts and congratulations and the buffet, the DJ kicks it up and everybody moves to the lawn to dance. Laurie and Brett are in the midst of it all, making up their own dance moves and laughing hysterically.

I've danced with Jordan, Brett's partner at the gym, with Dylan, and Chelsea, who arrived early and joined us upstairs in Laurie's bedroom. An assortment of Laurie's colleagues also come - cute lawyerly types with nice haircuts and tattoos that wouldn't be visible if they were wearing suits. One of them, I'm not sure which one, even slipped a card into my hand and asked me to call him to hang out sometime.

I take a sip from my fruit punch and watch the rest of the party from my place on a lawn chair, studiously ignoring Laurie's calls to come back and dance. Now that I'm tired, it's easy for my mind to return to Landon. I've tried my best to enjoy myself, but it's still hard to look at Laurie and Brett with the knowledge that it will never be Landon and me announcing our love to the world, and that it was always ridiculous to hope.

"Hey." It's one of the guys from Laurie's office, Brad or Tatum? He's new, so I'm not quite sure. He grins and takes the chair beside mine. "You're not dancing," he states.

He has beautiful dimples, and he's probably nice too. For some reason, that thought makes me sad. I think it's the realization that Landon has ruined me for every other guy, no matter how cute, or nice. "I'm a little tired," I reply.

"Okay." He's still smiling. "Laurie says you work at Gilt magazines."

"Yeah."

"I read the men's style mag sometimes," he tells me. "Must be interesting to work there."

"It is."

The conversation flags. On the lawn, everyone is still dancing. Had he been about to ask me to dance? I don't think I can bear another round of smiling and pretending to enjoy the music that's only making me feel lonelier than ever.

I get up and give him an apologetic smile. "I'm gonna fetch something," I murmur. "It was nice talking to you…"

"Jamie," he says. He smiles again and the dimples are heartbreakingly cute. "My name's Jamie."

I nod. "It was nice talking to you, Jamie."

After that, I walk away from the party, but I don't go

inside. Instead, I walk along the side of the house to the end of the garden, where there's a small white gazebo overlooking aunt Jacie's tulips. It's where she goes when she wants to read in the peace of the garden. Now, even with the noise of the party, the music and laughter, it's still somewhat peaceful.

Taking one of the seats inside, I draw up my legs, wrapping my arms around them and resting my chin on my knees.

Two weeks, and not even a single word.

I'd known the risk I was taking when I told Landon that I was in love with him, but still, I'd hoped that it would make him realize that he had feelings for me too. Now, it was obvious that he did not, that I'd probably always overestimated what I meant to him.

At times like this, my mind starts to run over everything he ever said to me. All the things that made me believe that what we had was special, that I wasn't the only one who had been drawn into the wild emotional vortex that was him and me.

But I was, obviously. While I'd been falling madly in love with him, he'd remained unscathed, able to walk away without looking back. While I was barely holding on to reason, he was perfectly able to let me go, and go on, with maybe only a few regrets.

He was Landon Court, after all, and he didn't do commitment.

Taking a deep breath, I close my eyes. I can't keep waiting for him. It's clear now, more than anything, that I have to move on with my life. I have to forget him.

My heart rebels against the thought, giving in to the aching feeling that follows it. I don't want to move on. I want to hold on to my memories and my feelings. I want to live on them for as long as I can, because as strong as I've tried to be, the thought of a life without Landon makes me want to hide somewhere and cry my heart out.

A gentle breeze rustles the trees surrounding the garden, and I hug myself tighter, letting a single tear drip slowly down my cheek. One day, I'll stop the self-immolation and move on with my life, but for now, I just want to think about Landon, to remember what it was like to be with him.

"Rachel."

I stiffen at the sound of the familiar voice, sure that I've only imagined it, and yet, desperately hopeful that it's real. I don't want to move, I don't want to turn around to look, for fear that he won't be there, that my desire for him has conjured him as a tortuous trick on my mind, and I'll see only the flowers in the garden, not Landon.

In the long silence that follows, I only hear the distant sounds of the party, the rustling of the leaves, and the pounding rhythm of my heart.

"Your mother told me you'd be back here," I hear the uncertainty in his voice. I loosen my arms from around my knees and drop my feet to the ground. I turn around slowly, tightening my fingers around the edge of the bench, because even after hearing his voice, I'm still not sure.

At the sight of him, my eyes water, but I let them rove over him, hungrily taking in the tousled, burnished hair, and his beautiful face, now clouded by a tentative frown. His body looks perfect in a dark jacket over a crisp white shirt and dark trousers, and the tender expression in his eyes washes over me like a soft wave.

"Landon?" My voice is shaky, my mind still unable to wrap itself around the thought that he's actually here.

"Hi." He tries on a small smile, but it quickly fades from his lips, and I hear him breathe heavily. My own chest tightens. "I hope you don't mind if I join you."

I close my eyes, and when I open them again, he's

still there. “No,” I say softly. “No, I don’t.”

3

Landon comes to join me on the bench. His shirt brushes my arm as he sits, making a slight tremor course through me. I look at his face, trying to fight the wild hope that's making it difficult for me to breathe.

He's watching me, silent, his eyes searching mine. In the silence, I wonder what he came here to say. My fingers tighten around the edge of the bench and I look away from his face. For all I know, he could be here to dash my last remnants of hope.

I hear him breathe, and I turn toward him just in time to see him reach into his jacket pocket and pull something out. He hands it to me. It's a single rose. Red and heartbreakingly lovely.

I take it from him, my hand shaking as I study the beautiful petals. "I didn't know you were coming," I tell him, still looking at the rose.

"I wasn't… I tried to call you. You weren't picking up. Laurie told me about the party, and that you were here."

"My phone's in the house," I explain.

He nods. "I guessed."

I swallow, still looking down, almost unable to bear the fact that he's seated right next to me. I can feel his nearness in every inch of my skin. It feels like a burning ache in my blood, like torture in my heart.

Closing my eyes, I place the rose on the bench beside me. Two weeks of silence. Two weeks without a single word. I don't even know what to say to him.

"Why did you come?"

Landon doesn't reply. I look at him again, and there's something about the way his eyes reach into mine. It makes me want to tell him not to bother with explanations, with speaking. It makes me want to close the space between us and lay my head against his chest. It annoys me, how ready I am to forgive his silence, how ready I am to fall back into his arms, after all the pain of the past two weeks.

"Rachel." He whispers my name, and my eyes start to fill. He takes my hand, and the touch singes my skin. I pull my fingers out of his grip and get up from the bench, folding my arms around my body in a useless gesture of defense. "Don't touch me," I croak.

"Rachel…"

"Two weeks, Landon," I whisper. "I waited for you…"

"Rachel," he says again. "Come back."

I shake my head. "I told you I was in love with you and you let me stew in your silence for two fucking weeks. Do you have any idea how hard it was for me to open up to you about my feelings?"

He rises to his feet, suddenly dwarfing me. "You left," he bites out, keeping his voice low.

I close my eyes, feeling the sting of tears. "Yes, and I'm sorry. I'm sorry I walked away when I said I wouldn't. It hurt me to leave you Landon, but I had to. It was clear that even though I told you how I felt, you were still holding back."

"So, as usual, you decided to walk away."

The accusation in his voice makes me frustrated and sad. "I couldn't wait around for you to decide that you didn't want me!"

He sighs, then closes his eyes and takes a deep

breath. "Please come back. Sit. Let's talk."

I look at his face. Not sure that I want to hear what he's going to say. The words I want to hear, he could have said already if he wanted to, and if he's only going to break my heart all over again, then I'd rather not listen.

I swallow the lump in my throat. "I don't think…"

"Rachel, for God's sake! For once, will you stop fighting me?"

From the expression on his face, I realize that he's only a second from lifting me bodily and dumping me on the bench, so I take the few steps back and lower myself to the seat. Landon sits beside me, his body angled toward mine.

"Look at me," he says firmly.

I lift my eyes to his, and a sigh almost escapes my lips. Why does he have to look so good? Even my nose is filled with the familiar scent of his skin, and my head with the memory of his touch. My eyes fill again, and he curses, reaching inside his pocket for a handkerchief, which he dabs at my tears.

After he puts the mascara stained cloth back in his pocket, he reaches for my hands, and this time I don't pull back. "These past two weeks. I've been… I don't know what I've been doing." He stops. "I didn't know.

I didn't know why you walked away before. I didn't know how you felt. I didn't know you thought you needed to get away from me. I didn't know your feelings made you believe you needed to get over me, or that my behavior, pursuing you relentlessly, ignoring your requests for me to leave you alone, took away the space you needed to do that." He looks at me. "I understand now. I get it. I get why you walked away that first time."

I look from his face to my hands, nestled in his. I don't know for sure if it's my hands trembling, or his. I stay silent, waiting for him to continue.

"I've been trying," he expels a harsh breath. "I've been trying to stop thinking about you. When I woke up and you had gone, I… I wanted to come after you, Rachel, you have no idea what it took to stay back and let you have the space I didn't give you in the past."

I told you I was in love with you, I say silently. I didn't want space. I wanted you to tell me that you felt the same way. Why would he even assume that I wanted space? And if that's what he thought, why was he here?

I hear the sound of his breath, and I feel his fingers tighten around mine, then loosen. He strokes my fingers gently, and when I raise my eyes to his face, he looks up too, into my eyes.

"There were so many times I wanted to come to

you," he says gently. "There were so many things I could have said, but Rachel, the last thing I wanted was for you to think I was telling you what you wanted to hear just so I get you to stay."

I close my eyes. I wasn't unaware how easy it was for some men to lie about how they felt, just to get what they wanted, but Landon wasn't that sort of man. He would never make me believe that he felt more than he did, just to keep me hanging on to him. "I didn't tell you I was in love with you because I wanted you to say some meaningless words back to me." My voice is tight, almost breaking. "I told you because it was the truth. If you don't feel the same way, I totally understand, I really do."

"Will you let me finish?" He's frowning now. "I've been trying to make sense of a lot of things. My feelings, yours… I was trying to make the best decision for both of us, trying to determine the right course of action… I didn't want to pester you as I had in the past. So I decided to wait a while, but then you told Joe you didn't want him picking you up anymore, I thought… I didn't know what to think."

"I didn't want to be reminded…"

"Of me?" His eyes search mine.

"Yes."

He nods slowly.

"Joe's presence reminded me every day that even though you knew how I felt, you chose to stay away."

He is silent. "I'm here now."

I breathe, filling lungs that are suddenly aching and tight. "Why?" My voice is only slightly higher than a whisper.

"Because I couldn't wait anymore. I'm crazy about you, Rachel. I've always known that much. I've always known that I wanted to be with you, that I'd protect you, that I'd give you anything you wanted, that I could never let you go."

I blink back tears and start to pull my hands from his, but he holds on to them.

"I knew all that, but I'd never allowed myself to think about love, being in love. I've never wanted it. I never thought it was for me. I grew up in the devastation that kind of emotion can cause, and so I…" He stops and leans toward me, bringing his face closer to mine, "Then you told me how you felt, and it took me by surprise. I'd wasted so much time being jealous of your ex, being insecure about why you wanted to be with me, why you always walked away. I never thought it was possible that you had those kind of feelings for me."

God! I'd loved him for so long, and he'd had no idea. I sigh. "And after I told you?"

He releases a low chuckle. "I was shocked. But more than that, even though I was so fucking scared of doing something wrong and hurting you. The fact that you felt that way about me... I can't begin to explain how it made me feel. Happy, humbled, elated, and afraid. That night, I could have responded and told you that I felt the same way, and now I know that it wouldn't have been a lie. At the time, I was afraid that you would leave, and I didn't want to say those words just as a way to make you stay.

I don't want to hope. My hands are trembling in his, and I wish they would stop, I wish my whole body would stop shaking. "What about now?"

He sighs. "I've been trying to take control of my feelings, trying to define them, to escape the… the vulnerability that comes with knowing that I'd give up everything else to make you stay, but the truth is, deep down, I've always known in a part of me, that there would never be anyone else for me."

I close my eyes, letting the words soak into my body. When I look at him again, his eyes are on my face. "I think I've been a fool for a very long time," he says, lifting one hand to smooth a stray strand of hair and tuck it behind my ear. "I've been in love with you for a while now. A long while."

Something starts to unfurl inside me, like a flower, like a nimbus of happiness. I want to melt into him, to throw myself into his arms… My chest swells. "Tell me," I breathe softly.

His throat works. "I don't want to be without you," he says. "I want us to make this work. I love you, Rachel. I'm helplessly, hopelessly in love with you."

A tear rolls down my cheek, quickly followed by another, and then a chuckle escapes my lips, because I'm so damn happy I feel like I'm going to burst. I realize that I'm grinning stupidly at him through my tears, and he's smiling back.

"I love you," he says again, and this time he puts an arm around me and draws me to him. "I love you," he whispers in my ear, before kissing my cheek.

I turn my face and touch my lips to his, breathing in the scent of his skin and sighing at the feel of his firm lips on mine. "I hate you for leaving me adrift these past two weeks," I tell him.

"But?" his voice is teasing, but his eyes are hopeful, digging into mine.

"But I love you, Landon."

He breathes, and then we're just sitting in each

other's arms, kissing, and watching the stars in the night sky, and it feels wonderful, beautiful to just sit there, so close, and so happy.

"I'm glad you came," I whisper.

His arm tightens around me. "I couldn't have stayed away." He draws back to look in my face. "I've seen you, every day I've been in town, and if you knew how hard it was for me not to reach out to you, then you'd know I'm never going a day without you by my side."

"You've been stalking me."

His smile is unrepentant. "It's not such a large city," he says cryptically. "And I wouldn't call it stalking… just taking longer detours to work so I can see you at least once, every day."

"Stalking," I insist, smiling as I remember all those times when I'd thought I saw a familiar car, or felt that quiver that made me believe he was near. He probably was. He'd never actually left me.

I close my eyes and lean into his body. There's still a lot we have to work on. We still have to learn to trust each other, to build a real relationship out of the way we feel, but I know we can make it work.

We sit there for a long time, his kisses sweet on my face and my hair, and his hand stroking my back. This is happiness, I think silently, exultantly. It's loving, and knowing that you're loved in return. With Landon, I feel as if I've finally found exactly where I belong.

Later, I steal a glance in the direction of the party. The music is still playing, and I can still hear voices and laughter. "You can't come all this way to a party and not get to dance," I tell Landon.

He follows my gaze, then laughs, and the happiness I hear in his voice mirrors mine. "Well, come on then," he says, getting up. He takes my hand and pulls me to my feet, and we walk arm in arm to join the rest of the party.

There's something magical about holding on to Landon and swaying slowly to the music even as the party ebbs around us. I can hear people leaving. The loud goodbyes and congratulations, but I don't care. I just want to remain in Landon's arms forever.

"Whose engagement party is this?" Laurie asks playfully, coming to join us in the middle of the lawn. "We're leaving," she tells me, when she gets my attention, "though I doubt that you'd notice."

My head is still on Landon's chest. "Say bye to Brett for me, and congratulations."

She holds out her arms and I step out of Landon's arms to give her a hug. She's spending the night at Brett's, something that's going to become permanent when she completes her move to his apartment.

"Take care of my cuz," she tells Landon. There's a warning note in her voice, but her eyes are shining.

I look up at Landon just as he smiles, and as usual, it's devastating. My heart flutters, and for a moment, I can't believe how happy, how lucky I am. "You know I will," he tells Laurie.

"Alright then," she says. We hug again, then she does a small wave and returns to the house.

I move back into Landon's arms. "You should be leaving too."

"Should I?" His hands circle my waist and pull me close. "I'm thinking of ways to convince you to come with me."

I giggle. "My parents expect me to spend the night with them, but I'll be back in the city tomorrow."

He leans forward to place a kiss on my forehead. "You'd better," he whispers.

There's a whole wealth of promise in his voice, and a small quiver of anticipation floods through me. I close my eyes, filling my senses with his nearness. We stay swaying on the lawn until the song ends, and the DJ gives us an apologetic smile as he switches off and starts to pack up his equipment. Inside the house, Laurie and Brett are already gone, and Dylan is passed out in the den. Landon says goodbye to Laurie's parents and mine after thanking them for a wonderful party.

"We were glad to have you," Auntie Jacie tells him. From her smile, it looks like she's already planning another engagement party in her head, and the thought of planning a future with Landon no longer makes me feel hopeless, because now I know he loves me.

"We'll be leaving in a few minutes," my mom reminds me as I follow Landon to the front door, almost as if she's afraid that I'll choose that moment to elope with him.

"I'll be right back," I tell her.

"Outside, Landon's car is parked across the street from the house, under the trees that line the lawns. A few petals have fallen off the trees onto the hood of his car, and the breeze shifts them across the gleaming metal.

We reach the car and Landon leans on the side, with me standing in front of him. He cups my chin and raises my face to his, his blue eyes roving over every inch as if he's trying to burn every one of my features into his memory. "God, I've missed you!" he murmurs.

I wrap my arms around him. "I've missed you too."

He drops a kiss on my forehead then trails a path of sweet kisses down to my nose. It tickles and I pull back, laughing. He's laughing too, and there's an expression on his face that looks like the bliss I'm feeling, and it warms me up inside. "I love you, Rachel Penelope Foster," he says with a laugh and a small shake of his head. "You won't believe how happy saying that makes me feel. It's as if I've been lying to myself and I can finally say the truth."

I grin. "Well, I love that you love me, Landon Alexander Court, and I love you too."

He chuckles. "Now I'm even happier than I was a moment ago."

My eyes close as my chest expands with almost uncontainable joy, and Landon pulls me back into the circle of his arms. "I love you," he whispers again, right before his lips take mine.

It starts soft and sweet, a teasing, caressing pressure on my lips that floods my heart with warmth. I kiss him back, wanting nothing more than to surrender myself to his touch. His hands move across my back, pressing me closer to his hard body while the kiss deepens. His tongue plunges into my mouth, caressing mine and flooding my body with a wild, pulsing heat.

He pulls back after a moment, leaving me panting and breathless. He's breathing deeply too, grinning as he looks down at me. "I'll see you tomorrow," he says, his voice dark with sensual promise.

My breath catches. "I can't wait."

He waits in the car, making sure I'm almost at the door before he starts to drive away. Inside the house, Dylan is still dozing on the couch in the den, but my mother is packing things up in the kitchen.

"Well, at least you didn't leave with him," she remarks. I can't tell if the expression on her face is disapproval or the opposite. Aunt Jacie gives her a look before smiling at me.

"Well, I was glad to see you looking alive for the first time all weekend."

"I've been looking alive," I protest halfheartedly. "I'm just tired. Work and everything."

"Hmm." She doesn't sound convinced.

"Can I help?"

My mom shakes her head. "Go find your dad. Tell him we're leaving."

My dad and Uncle Taylor are in the study bent over their unending chess game. It's not really endless, they just start another game as soon as someone wins, so there's always a game going on.

"Hey dad, Uncle T," I call from the door.

"Time to go?" My dad looks regretful. As he gets up, he wags a finger at his twin. "Don't cheat," he warns Uncle Taylor.

"Never," Uncle Taylor replies, winking at me. They both cheat, which is why no one else will play with them.

We go back to the den and wake Dylan, then my mother joins us from the kitchen, and we hug our goodbyes before heading to the car, where Dylan goes straight to sleep again.

It's a short drive, and my mother keeps up the conversation, talking about everything from the music to the caterer, to family friends with little kids who had grown up fast.

At home, Dylan goes to bed. My dad too, but my mom follows me up to my old room, wondering aloud about the arrangements for Laurie's wedding, how little time we have to prepare, if we'll have to import the flowers from home or procure them in Bridgetown… I listen to her chatter, waiting for her to say what's really on her mind.

Once we're in the bedroom, she goes to sit on the edge of the bed. "So, Laurie's moving out," she starts. "You'll find another roommate won't you? So you won't be alone? I've heard that singles thrive better when they have roommates."

"Ha ha," I smile. "I haven't decided. Maybe I'll enjoy living alone."

"Okay." She shrugs. "It's so nice to have you here." There's nostalgia in her eyes. "You haven't been home much these past few weeks."

"I miss you too mom, all the time." I laugh. "Feel free to invite me to any 'art' things you have in the city."

"So you can run away with Landon Court like you did the last time."

I don't reply, so she continues. "Sweetie, I don't want to be worried about you, especially since you seem so happy, but are you sure he's the right person for you?"

I join her on the bed. We'd talked when I was insecure about Landon's feelings for me, so I don't blame her for her concern.

"Mom, I'm in love with him."

"I can see that." She sighs. "You already told me as much anyway. But what about him? Does he share your feelings?"

Does he love me?

I smile because there's no longer any doubt in my mind. "He feels the same way," I tell my mom, pleasure bubbling inside me again. "He feels the same way."

She nods, leaning forward to touch a finger to my cheek. "You should always feel safe in your relationship, and you should be extremely sure of the person you love. Committing to someone is the most important decision you'll ever make, and it can either take you to places you want to go or it can destroy you."

"Mom!" I exclaim, laughing. "You are not speaking from experience."

"How do you know?" she laughs. "Maybe I led a dangerously adventurous life before I fell in love with your dad."

I raise a dubious brow and she sighs. "Okay, you're right, I'm not speaking from experience, not mine anyway," she admits. "But be careful, okay? I don't want you to give too much of yourself and end up getting hurt."

"Don't worry, Mom." I give her a reassuring smile. "Landon is one of the good ones."

"Yes, but a man like him… wealthy, busy, with so many responsibilities… I just hope he'll give you the time and attention to ensure you never feel…"

"Unimportant?" I supply with a raised brow.

"I was going to say neglected," she amends.

"Whichever one… just don't worry about me. I'll be

fine. We'll be fine."

"Alright then. You're old enough to know what you're doing." She gets up and gives me one last concerned look. "Good night, sweetheart."

"Night, mom."

When she's gone, I shower and change into my nightclothes. I'm about to call Landon when my phone rings. My whole body flushes with pleasure when I see his name on my screen.

"Are you home?" I ask.

"Yes, just got here. Are you in bed?"

"Yes."

"You should have come with me," he says. "Say you will and I'll come right back to get you."

"No," I laugh. "You waited two weeks, what's one more day."

"I'll make you forget about those two weeks. I promise you that."

My skin flushes. "Knowing your methods, can I just say I'm looking forward to that?"

He laughs. "Say anything, baby. When I get you here tomorrow, the only thing you'll be saying is my name."

"Maybe I'll run away," I tease.

"I'll find you." He sounds serious. "No matter where you go."

"I love you," I say softly.

I can almost hear the smile in his voice. "I love you too."

4

Monday morning, I go to work directly from my parent's place, and after the crazy traffic and grumpy cabdriver, I finally reach the office just in time to avoid clocking in late.

I smile at the interns on the elevator and throw a friendly greeting at the receptionist on my floor. Even Carole Mendez, my editor-in-chief's dragon-like secretary gets a smile from me when I pass her in the hall. I can't believe how happy I am. I feel as if I'm floating.

Minutes after I enter my office, there is a knock and a delivery of the most beautiful arrangement of flowers ever. I retrieve the card, excited as I read Landon's message.

'Have a great start to your week,' it says. *'You own my heart.'*

I close my eyes, my hand going to my mouth as my heart floods with overwhelming emotion.

Picking up my phone, I go to my last call and dial his number, and he picks on the first ring.

"Hey, love."

"Hey, yourself." I'm grinning like an idiot. "I got your flowers."

"I hope you like them?"

"Are you seriously asking that?" I sigh. "Of course I love them."

I hear him breathe. "How's it going over there?"

"I just got to work. Nothing yet."

"I have this crazy desire to cancel my entire schedule for the day, come over, and steal you away," he says. "I have a meeting in a few minutes, but I'm busy scrolling through pictures of you on my phone."

My heart swells. "What pictures?"

"The ones from the beach in Newport," he replies with a self-mocking laugh. "They've been my constant companions these past two weeks."

I remember that particular weekend, the Sunday

afternoon we spent on the beach walking and taking selfies and I suddenly miss him with my whole being. "I want to cancel my schedule too," I admit. I feel like I would be happy to shirk all my other roles, be his girlfriend and nothing else for as long as possible. It's a silly thought, disloyal to all notions of female independence, but it's born out of a profound and indescribable happiness. "I have to wean myself off you," I say with a sigh. "I'm afraid of how totally you've captivated me."

"Don't even dare." Landon laughs softly. "Though I'm sure I'm the one who's helplessly captivated."

"I can't wait for this evening," I whisper.

There is a short silence on his end. "This time, I'm never letting you go."

I close my eyes. "I'm not going anywhere. Never again."

"I'm thinking up reasons to postpone this meeting so we can keep talking," he admits.

"What's the meeting about?"

"Does it matter?" There is a smile in his voice. "Actually it's to discuss a conceptual design proposal for a property I want to acquire in Vegas."

"I read about that."

"So you were reading about me."

I smile. "Stop teasing."

"I kept all the articles that had pictures of us together. You looked lovely in all of them."

I close my eyes, not sure of how to reply to that. "Thanks," I say finally.

He chuckles. "You're welcome,"

"I have an interview today," I tell him, explaining about the invitation from the Gilt Review.

"Does that happen often?" His voice is serious. "An interview from such an old application?"

I think of Gertrude Weyland, and Jack's certainty that his mother had something to do with the whole situation, but until I confirmed it, I couldn't say for sure.

"I've never heard of anything like that happening here at Gilt, but I'm not going to let that stop me from going for it. It's what I've always wanted."

"Well, that's good," Landon says, "and you deserve it." There's a short pause. "I really can't wait to see you tonight."

I breathe softly, my fingers hovering over the soft petals of the flowers on my desk. I love him with an intensity that's verging on desperation, and at that moment, it makes me almost afraid, because if anything happened, if anything changed, if I lost him again, I have no idea how I would bear it.

"I'm counting down the hours," I tell him, making an effort to push all my fears aside. Nothing will go wrong, not if we're both committed to building our relationship. I know I am, and I know that Landon is too.

Landon ends the call so he can start his meeting, and I inhale the sweet scent of the flowers before settling at my desk, wondering what I could send to him in return. I'm starting up my computer when I get an idea. I pick up my phone again, this time calling Chadwick.

"I'm not mad," he says when he picks up. "First you break my heart, then you introduce me to your cousin and she finishes the job."

"Chadwick!" I laugh, "Your heart's the one in your chest, not the one in your pants."

"She didn't do anything with that one either."

"Come on." My voice is teasing, "You're Chadwick Black, there are probably a hundred girls waiting for you to give them a call right now."

He sighs. "How is she?"

I grimace. "Engaged."

"Perfect!" he says grumpily, "I talked her straight into another man's home and hearth."

"We are all very grateful for that."

"Well," he pauses, "What can I do for you?"

"Are you still in town?"

"Yes."

I tell him what I want, and by the time I'm done I can hear the excitement in his voice. "Of course," he tells me. "I'd even do that for free."

I purse my lips. "That won't be necessary."

"Okay," he accepts. We make arrangements, and as I imagine what Landon's reaction will be when I give him my gift, I can't keep the excited smile off my face.

My interview is set for late in the afternoon, before then, I manage to sneak out to keep my appointment with Chadwick. Back in the office, I fix my appearance and take a deep breath. Gilt Review is only two floors above us, so I take the stairs, and by the time I get there, I'm nervous as hell, but also very hopeful.

I'll get the job, I tell myself, somehow sure that it's my week of serendipity.

The offices remind me a lot of Gilt Travel. It's the same layout, and most of the people are regular, literary types, not like the fashion gods and goddesses at Gilt Style. One of the receptionists leads me to the conference room, and I wave at some of the people I know when I see them in the corridor. They're probably wondering what I'm doing here. I imagine they'll find out soon, and then it won't be long before my colleagues downstairs find out, then my boss, Jessica Layner will surely hear about it. I smother the little sliver of dread. Jessica would probably have something to say about me interviewing for Review, something I might not like to hear, but I'm not going to let that stop me.

My interviewer is a woman in her mid-thirties, with a tired smile and a deep, husky voice. She introduces herself as Liz Buckley, the senior editor I'd spoken with earlier. For the interview, she asks me the typical questions, why I applied to the Review, what I think I can contribute, then we start to talk about the authors and stories recently published in the magazine, and since I'm a faithful reader, I know almost every issue by heart. She starts to look less bored, and after an animated discussion, she tells me to expect a call.

I get up and shake her hand. "May I ask why I got this invitation," I ask, not wanting to leave without clearing that up at least. "It's been two years since I applied."

She looks surprised, as though she thought I would know. "We reviewed your application and decided you'd be a good fit," she says.

I frown, knowing how unlikely that was. "Okay."

She starts to pack up her things, leaving me no choice but to do the same. On my way back to my office, I decide to stop wondering and allow myself to feel good about the fact that I might just get the job I've always wanted.

As soon as I get back to the office, Landon calls.

"How did it go?"

"Good. I think I have a good chance."

"You are great at what you do," he says encouragingly. "I'm sure they can see that. And if they don't, I'll have to buy the whole company and make you the publisher."

"Ha Ha," I laugh softly. "The entire Gilt Publications! I doubt they'd let you buy it, and I don't want to be the boss. I just want to read stories for a living."

"I envy you," he says. "So, when will you be done over there?"

"In about an hour."

"Good. Joe will be on his way to pick you up. He'll bring you to the office. Is that okay? Or do you want to go to the apartment?"

"No, I'll come over." I'm so eager to see him that the thought of waiting alone in the apartment is not appealing.

"Good then." He pauses. "I should go now, and try to get some work done, finally."

I laugh. "What have you been doing all day?"

"I've been thinking about your body and what I'd like to do with it. It's been like an erotic movie playing in my head all day. Very distracting."

A long sigh escapes me. I feel the same way, hot and bothered… it had been two weeks, after all.

"Can't you think of dead leaves or something," I joke weakly.

"I doubt that will work," Landon says. "Wait…I'm picturing dead leaves right now. Ah!… no. Didn't work. I still have a hard-on."

My imagination goes into overdrive. The thought of him, hard, in my hands, in my mouth… it fills me with a fierce, uncontrollable lust. "You're distracting me," I complain. "How am I supposed to work?"

"Good thing you were about to leave."

"I said in an hour. I'm not leaving now. I have work to do. I'm very busy and important, and in very high demand."

"Yes, you are." I'm sure he's smiling. "I love you."

"I love you too," I reply with a sigh. No matter how many times he says those words, the novelty, the beauty of hearing them from him will never go away.

"Now, I'm going to force myself to study a contract for the next hour. I'll see you soon."

It takes some effort to go back to my work after that, but I do my best. However, all I can think about is the many things I know Landon is going to do to my body later.

Joe is waiting for me when I get downstairs. Taciturn as usual, he drives me over to the SCT building, Landon's downtown high-rise. As I take the steps up to the entrance, my body is filled with anticipation. In the lobby, the security at the front desk hands me a visitor badge to enable me cross the turnstiles and waves me toward the elevators.

On Landon's floor, the receptionist presses a button to open the glass security doors for me, before giving me a small polite smile.

"Do you know the way?" she asks.

"Yes, thank you."

My mind goes briefly to the last time I was here, and I can't prevent a smile at the memories. I'd been struggling then, intent on making sure I didn't give in to my attraction to Landon, and now here I am, in love with him, and the best part is that he feels the same way.

Tony Gillies meets me at the outer office. He's Landon's assistant, or senior assistant, as there are at least two others on the team. "Great to see you," he says with a grin.

"Hello, Tony." The last time I saw him he was running around trying to make sure the opening of the Gold Dust Hotel went smoothly. He looks less stressed now. The other desks in the office are empty, and I assume the others have closed for the day. Tony motions for me to go straight into Landon's office before going back to his seat.

I take a deep breath as I approach the opaque glass doors, anticipation making me nervous. Inside, Landon is seated at his desk. He's not wearing his jacket, only a dark gray shirt that somehow sets off the burnished gold in his hair. He looks up when I enter, his face lighting up with a smile as he rises to his feet.

"Hello." His eyes rove over me, obvious hunger in their blue depths.

I round the desk, walking eagerly into his ready arms. They go around me, and I rest my head on his chest, inhaling his scent, filling all my senses with him. "Hey, Handsome."

He steps back to study me, a small smile on his lips. "Have I told you how sexy you look in office clothes?" He runs a hand down the front of my blouse. "You should come work here. As anything you like, just so I can look at you all day."

"Very empowering," I reply, quivering at his touch. "You're obviously plotting my expulsion from the women's movement.'

A ringing phone interrupts the beautiful and carefree sound of his laughter, and he reaches for one of the desk phones, motioning for me to sit in his chair. "I need to take this," he tells me, sounding apologetic.

I shrug my permission, and he leans his hip on the desk, his eyes on me while he talks to whoever's on the other end. I place my bag on his desk, and then, holding his gaze with a teasing look in my eyes, I drop to my knees in front of him.

The slight stammer in his voice when I start to undo his zipper makes me look up at him with a smile. He recovers quickly, continuing his conversation while I pull down his briefs. He's already hard, growing harder as I enclose him with my fist.

His skin is warm and satiny smooth. Silk pulled tight over hard steel. I stroke him up and down, loving the feel of him in my hand. Leaning forward, I cover the tip of his cock with my lips, flicking my tongue around the broad head. He's still talking, his voice steady. I meet his eyes and feel his hip muscles tense. He covers the receiver. "Don't stop," he whispers.

As if I would! I pull him deep into my mouth, till he's touching the back of my throat, then I draw my tongue along the underside of his cock, before moving my lips back up to surround his tip. When I look up at him again, his hand is clenched around the receiver, with the other hand curled around the edge of the desk, his knuckles almost white.

I release him from my mouth, licking my lips as I stroke him up and down, using the moisture from my mouth and the pre-cum seeping out of him to rub him from the root to the tip.

Landon holds the receiver away from his face and throws his head back, a soft moan escaping his lips. His cock is hard and pulsing against my hand, his look of helplessness and stark arousal contrasting with his unmistakable masculine strength.

He moans again, and I revel in the heady feeling of power the sound gives me. I stroke him harder and faster, watching as he brings the receiver back to his ear and starts to talk again. I hear the tinny sound as the person on the other end responds, and I take him back in my mouth, watching his tortured frown as he concentrates on maintaining the conversation. I suck him deep, and then start to move my head, faster and faster, hollowing my cheeks, tightening my lips around him. The hand on the desk reaches into my hair, the fingers tangling into the strands. I cup his balls, stroking them softly without reducing my pace.

"Ensure that you get back to me," I hear him bite into the phone, his voice curt and dismissive. I imagine the hapless person on the other end thinking that he's done something to annoy the boss. "Tomorrow at the latest."

He doesn't wait for the person to say anything else. He hastily puts down the receiver and lets out a long, heavy groan.

"Ah... fuck!"

I keep my pace. A soft moan escapes me when his fingers tighten in my hair, holding my head in place while he flexes his hips, driving back and forth into my mouth, the underside of his cock sliding against my tongue and bottom lip.

"Fuck," he moans. "Fuck! Rachel."

I stroke his thighs, feeling the muscles bunch and tighten.

"So good," he groans harshly. "So fucking good."

I moan in reply, sucking and licking him while raising my eyes to his. He lets out another harsh groan, his hips jerking as he reaches his release, coming with a burst of warmth inside my mouth.

He's shaking. His hand leaves my hair, smoothing it gently before he leans back on the desk. "Oh my God!" he breathes.

I suck in my bottom lip, still tasting him. Getting back on my feet, I take the chair he offered me earlier. "What can I say?" I tease, "I missed you very much."

He expels a deep breath, dragging his hands through his hair as he blinks at me. "I'm overwhelmed. Give me a minute to gather my mental faculties."

"Overwhelmed?" I grin playfully. "I guess I'm good like that."

Landon's eyes narrow, and he drops down to his knees in front of me. "Guess what," he whispers softly. "So am I."

I breathe in anticipation, watching him as he reaches for the buttons of my blouse. "I want you naked," he murmurs. "I want to see your beautiful body." He undoes the buttons one by one then pushes the front of the blouse apart. My bra fastens in front, and Landon's lips curve as he undoes the hooks, freeing my breasts.

My nipples peak under the intense consideration of

his eyes, extending even further when he flicks his thumbs over the sensitive peaks.

"I missed these," he murmurs, squeezing a nipple between the thumbs and forefingers of each hand. "You have such beautiful breasts."

The combination of his voice and his touch is so sexy, I let out a small moan, and he chuckles, leaving my nipples to unfasten my skirt and pull it down, along with my panties. He spreads my legs over the arms of the chair so I'm totally exposed, open to his gaze.

I'm already so aroused from watching him come, that my body is eager, wet, pulsing, and he can tell.

Landon draws a finger from my navel down between my legs, and then rubs me gently, spreading the wetness across my folds, from my swollen clit down to my wet opening. He strokes the pulsing entrance to my body, making me moan his name as pleasure courses through me. When he slides two hooked fingers inside me, my body clenches around them, tightening with desire as he starts to move them in and out. He's watching my face as the sensations build, and I groan, rolling my hips when he finds the clump of sensitive nerves inside me and starts to stroke it in slow, sweet circles.

The feeling of arousal is intense, and all the muscles in my body strain harshly as his touch brings me closer and closer to orgasm. My hips move in time with his fingers, wanting to feel more.

"Landon," I moan.

"What?" His voice is soft and husky. Pure sex and unrelenting temptation.

"Ah…" I moan again, incapable of coherent thought, of forming sentences. Still stroking me inside, he lowers his lips to my clit, nuzzling then flicking his tongue across the sensitive bud. I respond with a soft cry, the sweetness of his touch taking over my senses. His tongue continues to move, fast, yet light and teasing, pulling my pleasure out of the deepest parts of my body.

I almost tip the chair over when I come, my hips buck uncontrollably, and my cries are loud and abandoned as my body pulses with the force of my climax. I watch Landon rise to his feet with glazed eyes, almost uncomprehending as he lifts me from the chair and places me on the desk, my legs still spread. He stands between them, his beautiful cock fisted in his hand one moment, then in the next, he's sliding it deep inside me.

I release a long moan as he fills me, stretching me tight. I've missed this feeling, so much. My hips move restlessly, wanting more, and Landon is happy to oblige.

He leans his hands on the desk, his body curved over mine as he starts to pump into me, each firm thrust of his hips building the massive sensations taking over my body. His lips cover one of my nipples, sucking deeply on the erect bud even as he drives me to madness with the sweet strokes of his cock. I run my hands over his chest, crying out in sexual abandon. The sound of my moans fill the office as I meet his every stroke with an uninhibited thrust of my hips, far past the point of wanting anything but him, deeper inside me, giving me the pleasure only he can.

We come at the same time, our wild cries of pleasure merging and blending until I can't tell which sound is him and which is me. I fall back on the desk, hands stretched over my head, my body spread out like a willing sacrifice. I don't care. My breath is coming in short gasps, there's a sheen of sweat on my skin, and as he pulls out of me, a sound like a purr escapes my lips, my body shuddering with the aftershock of purest pleasure.

Landon collapses on his chair, making no attempt to fix his clothes. He rests his head on my still-trembling thighs, breathing deeply. "I think I like my desk with you on it, naked."

I manage a laugh. "Please don't joke. I can't respond right now. I'm recovering from a celestial event."

His laughter makes me feel warm inside. "Yeah, me too."

5

After we've fixed our clothes, we go up to the apartment he keeps above the office. Nothing has changed since the last time I was here, the first time we made love in his office. It's still as stark as I remember, an enormous difference from the larger and better decorated Swanson Court Hotel apartment.

Landon shows me to the master bedroom. It's a large room, spotlessly clean, but as Spartan as the rest of the apartment. I can totally see him, tired from work, coming up here just to crash and get ready for another workday.

"What do you do here when you're not asleep?" I ask, looking at the bare walls.

He spares a glance around the room and shrugs. "Sometimes I continue working. It's just an office with a bed, mostly."

"Yes, I can see that."

Landon points me in the direction of the bathroom, and while I freshen up, he selects a change of clothes from the sparsely populated closet.

Later, while I'm sitting on a corner of the soft bed waiting for him to change, a part of my mind starts to wonder if he has brought any other women here. In my mind's eye, I see Ava Sinclair's face from that night in San Francisco at the opening of the Gold Dust, her beautiful lips curved in a smirk, and I wonder if she was ever here, or at the Swanson Court apartment. It doesn't matter, I tell myself, pushing the jealous thoughts from my head. I'm the one Landon is in love with.

"What are you thinking?" He's standing at the door to the walk-in closet, wearing a beige V-neck sweater over a white shirt, with dark pants that display the slim length of his legs. He looks casual and sexy, and I want to put my arms around him, and somehow, I don't know how, join myself to him in a way that no one would ever be able to pull us apart.

"Nothing," I reply.

He raises an eyebrow, and I sigh. "I was just… I was

being silly, imagining you here with other women."

When Landon doesn't reply, I look up to meet his gaze, a shamefaced expression on mine, but he is smiling, and he comes to join me on the bed. "I don't think that's silly. I'd like for you to forget every single person who came before me as well."

I snort. Already forgotten, I say silently, and as if he knows what I'm thinking, he laughs. "For your information, no women here, ever. After my father died, I went through this period when I didn't want anything to do with the Swanson Court, I left home, got my own apartment… Somehow it's always made more sense to entertain my women friends there."

I understood why. He'd grown up at the Swanson Court apartment. It still held memories for him, and it might not have seemed right to share those memories with the many women he'd dated casually through the years.

But he'd shared them with me.

"Do you still have it?" I ask softly. "The apartment."

He shakes his head. "I sold it a few months ago. I knew I wouldn't need it anymore."

A few months ago. Long before I told him how I felt. His hand is on my lap, and I cover it with mine, sure, at that moment, that there is no reason to fear that anything would ever go wrong between us.

"In any case," Landon continues. "I'm planning to sell this place soon. I don't intend to spend as much time in the office as before, and it can serve a better purpose as part of the residential complex."

The SCT building was a mix of commercial office space and residential apartments, so this apartment could easily be added to the residential side. I study Landon's face, wondering what he means. Is he planning to spend more time with me, or is he going to be traveling more? I hope fervently that it's the former.

My stomach growls unexpectedly, reminding me that I'm hungry. Landon gives me a teasing grin. "I've already ordered dinner," he says, getting up and pulling me to my feet. The bell from the service elevator rings just as we enter the living room and Landon lets the person from the gourmet food-delivery service into the apartment.

The man makes a big deal out of laying out the food in the small dining room, and I'm relieved when he finally leaves. Dinner is playful and sensual. Landon feeds me, and I love the way his eyes glaze over when I lick my lips slowly, my eyes on his.

"You're such a tease," he tells me.

"You love it," I reply.

He laughs. "I love you."

I melt right there. I can't help it. "I love you too."

He's grinning. "I know."

Afterward, we put away the dishes and go back to the living room. There isn't much in the way of entertainment, a TV and a game console with access to a few subscription channels. I'm not really in the mood to do anything other than snuggle beside Landon on the couch, my body as close to him as possible, my head on his chest.

I start to drift off, and I'm already almost asleep when I hear him say my name, a soft whisper in my ear.

"Hmm," I reply.

"I should get you home."

"I don't want to go," I murmur, but I know I have to. I'd have preferred to go with him to his apartment at the hotel, but Laurie is spending the night at our place and I'd already agreed to meet her there.

I hear Landon chuckle softly. "We'll go out to dinner tomorrow. How about that?"

I burrow deeper into his arms. "Okay."

Joe is waiting to drive us to my apartment, and once there, Landon walks upstairs with me and gives me a deep, sensual kiss at the door, leaving me weak and wanting, before he says goodbye.

Inside the apartment, Laurie is still awake. She's in her room, packing up some of her clothes. She grins when she sees me.

"You look happy."

"I am happy," I reply, flopping on the bed. "Happy like a lovesick halfwit."

She snorts with laughter then wiggles her eyebrows at me. "I can imagine. You guys have probably exhausted all the Cosmo sex positions by now."

"Ugh." I shake my head. "You have such a dirty mind."

"Oh, I do?" She laughs. "So… You guys spend all your time together talking about books and TV shows?"

I stick out my tongue at her, then looking at the piles of folded clothes beside me on the bed, I frown in concern. "You think you'll be all ready by the weekend?"

She nods. "Yeah. It's mostly just clothes and books, plus a few knickknacks. I'll spend a few hours every day after work putting them together. I'll be done before Saturday."

I nod. "Where's Brett?"

"He left about an hour ago." She casts a wistful glance toward the bed and I wrinkle my nose and make a big show of shifting to the very edge.

"You're such a nympho!" I exclaim.

She grins and tosses a t-shirt at me.

"Are you apprehensive?" I ask softly, "about the wedding?"

She frowns. "About the wedding itself, or getting married to Brett?"

"I don't know… Both?"

She shrugs. "About Brett? No. I just feel at peace, you know? Happy. Like I know that this was always meant to happen, like I was always meant for him, for this. I'm a hundred percent sure about him."

"But?"

She pauses and frowns. "Sometimes, I fret about all the arrangements, the dress, how the pictures will turn out, guest lists and all that… but you know, all that matters is that at the end of the day, Brett and I say our vows and officially become the most important people in each other's lives."

"Plus your mom and mine are taking over the arrangements anyway, so no need to fret."

"Exactly." She looks at me, one eyebrow raised. "Why all the questions? Are you thinking of dragging poor Landon to the altar?"

"He wouldn't be poor Landon if I did," I say indignantly. "He'd be lucky."

"That is the spirit," Laurie grins.

"I wasn't really thinking about marriage. I was just… I don't know, wondering how you know for sure, without any doubts."

"Do you have doubts? About Landon?"

I shake my head. "I know he's the one." I pause. "I don't even know what he thinks about marriage as an institution, you know?" Especially with how his parents marriage had turned out.

"Well, considering what you've told me about his relationship with his brother, he'd probably be a great dad."

"We haven't cleared marriage and you're talking kids," I shake my head, although my mind dwells on the pleasant thought for a forbidden moment. Landon's kids, my kids. The idea is so tempting, too tempting. "I don't even know what I think about kids, except I'm sure I'll have at least one set of twins who'll be worse than our moms."

"That would be awful," Laurie replies, laughing. It's a joke between us that our moms act as if they're the twins in the family.

"I'll miss this place," Laurie says wistfully, her eyes going around the room. "Remember when we first moved in?"

"Yeah." We'd been so proud, and we'd attached so much importance to simple things like buying furniture. Now Laurie isn't even taking many of the things we purchased. Just her lamps and a few picture frames.

"I'll miss you," I tell her. "You and your damn reality shows."

"You know you love them," she teases.

I grin, "No, it's you I love."

"Awww." She makes a sad face. "I love you too."

We stay grinning at each other until I throw her t-shirt back at her and it lands on her face, then I help her pack until it's time to go to bed.

The next day I leave work and go directly to the Swanson Court Hotel. I'm having dinner with Landon, but we're leaving from his apartment. At the ground floor lobby, I make my way over to the elevators, remembering my impressions from the first time I ever came here. The beauty and tastefulness of the interior had impressed me, and months after, my admiration for the place hasn't changed.

The elevator deposits me in the foyer of Landon's apartment and when I get to the living room, I'm surprised to see him seated on one of the armchairs. He has glasses on and he's reading from a tablet. Wow! I think, staring, even the nerdy look is sexy on him.

"Hi!" I exclaim, delighted. "I didn't know you were home."

"I left early." He puts the tablet aside and pulls off the glasses before rising languidly to his feet. He comes toward me and slides his hands around my waist, holding me close while his lips find mine, overwhelming me with a sweet, welcoming kiss. "How was your day?"

"So, so." I grin, breathing in the scent of his skin mixed with that subtle and irresistible hint of cologne, and thinking expectantly of the few hours we have before we have to go out to dinner. "How was yours?"

Landon shrugs, and kisses me again, tasting my lips and teasing my tongue for a long sweet moment. When he pulls back, I moan softly, wanting more. He takes my bag off my shoulder, dropping it on one of the chairs. "What's that you're holding?"

"Oh." I look down at the small gift bag in my hand, suddenly nervous. Chadwick expedited my order and had it delivered to the office earlier in the day. "Ummm," I raise the bag, handing it to him. "It's for you."

His eyebrow quirks. "Really?" He takes it from me

and with his arm still around me, leads me to the sofa. He watches my face, a quizzical expression on his as he pulls the packages out, and carefully unwraps them. He studies the first one, then the second, while I wait for him to say something.

"I…" He shakes his head, and when he meets my gaze, his eyes are molten and wondrous. "These are incredibly beautiful."

I breathe, looking from his face to the picture frames. They're both small desk-size frames, and the photos they contain are black and white. The first one a very sensual shot of me lying on a chaise lounge, a sheet arranged over my body in such a way that it's clear that I'm wearing nothing underneath. The other one is more conservative. I'm fully dressed, but it's still a sexy pose.

"When you'd said you'd spent all that time looking at my pictures from the beach, I just thought… I wanted to…"

He stops me. "They're perfect. I could look at them all day."

I grin. "Which one in particular?"

"Both of them," He gives me a teasing smile. "Though…" His eyes go back to the first picture. "You have a dirty mind, don't you."

I chuckle, watching as he reluctantly tears his eyes from the frames and sets them down beside him. He pulls me into his arms. "I love your dirty mind," he says.

"And I love your dirty mouth, your dirty hands..." I dig my fingers into his silky hair, loving the feel of the lush strands.

He suddenly pulls back to look in my face. "Who took these?"

I raise a brow. "Does it matter?"

He chuckles. "My jealousy is so obvious, is it?"

"It's a little charming actually," I say with a shrug. "It was Chadwick Black. He's a photographer we work with at Gilt, and, before you ask, both his photographer's assistant and his PA were there throughout the shoot. Okay?"

"Okay." Landon laughs, then he rises suddenly, with me still in his arms. I place my arms around his neck for leverage while he carries me up the stairs to his bedroom. He sets me down on the bed and leans over me, reaching for the buttons on my top. "I've been thinking about undressing you all day."

I giggle. "I hope you managed to get some work done. Those hotels won't run themselves."

He smiles, pulling the top apart to expose my bra. "I tried."

I help him shrug it off my shoulders before reaching for his shirt and getting rid of that too. I run my fingers over his chest, trailing over the hard muscles. "How did you get to be so perfect?"

He smirks. "I was born this way?"

"You need to learn some humility," I say, pushing him back on the bed. He lays there, his head resting on his hands while I undo his fly. "Do you remember that first night?" I'm smiling. "Take off your clothes," I murmur, mimicking his voice, "all your clothes."

"Is that supposed to be me?" Landon laughs. "I don't sound like that." He raises his hips to help me pull down his pants. "I was trying my best to keep it cool that night. I wanted to devour you."

"You were hot," I confess.

He winks. "I know."

I toss his pants aside, then stretch out on top of him, my face on level with his. "I'm not going to make love to you if you keep talking like you're so smooth and perfect."

His hand caresses my back. "What if I beg?"

"I might reconsider."

He lifts his head and covers my mouth with his, slowly licking at the seam of my lips. I kiss him back, enjoying the feel of his lips, the taste of his mouth, his tongue, mating with mine. He rolls, still holding me, so that I'm beneath him, and releasing my lips, he undoes my skirt and pulls it down, tossing it in the direction I threw his discarded pants. He trails his hand up my thigh, playing with the lace edge of my panties before moving up to draw a line up the strap of my bra.

I raise my upper body off the bed to allow him to undo the undergarment, then lift my arms so he can pull it off me. He tosses it, and his eyes settle on my breasts. I love the way he looks at me, as if I'm the most beautiful person he has ever seen. It makes me feel more beautiful and loved than I ever thought it was possible to feel. He palms one of my breasts, his thumb flicking over the nipple, his eyes fixed on the pink bud as it hardens and peaks, the look of rapt attention on his face feeding every feeling of vanity inside me.

I raise myself from the bed, pushing him gently, so he falls on his back. "I want you like this," I whisper, reaching for his briefs and pulling them down his legs. I reach for him, feeling the warm, velvety hardness of his cock in my hands. He moans when I stroke him, a low sound from deep in his throat. Giving him a small smile, I lower my head to lick the head of his cock, swirling my tongue around it and luxuriating in his guttural moans of pleasure.

I pull him deep into my mouth and his eyes close, his fingers flexing on the bed. I suck him hard, loving the effect I have on him, the reactions my touch evokes. His hips flex and one hand reaches for my hair, his fingers smoothing the strands as he whispers encouragements.

"Just like that, baby,"

"Right there, Rachel."

"Oh, Fuck!"

I love the sound of his voice, the edge of arousal and helpless desire. Sucking hard on the head of his cock, I stroke my hand up and down his length, watching as his eyes close and his lips part. His feet press into the mattress and his hips start to move, encouraging me to take him deeper into my mouth. There's nothing as arousing as watching him come to pieces because of my touch.

"You're killing me," he groans harshly.

In response, I make my movements faster. I hear him curse, and in the next moment, he rears off the bed, pulling me off him and coming up behind me on his knees. He grabs hold of the waistband of my panties and pulls, getting them down to mid-thigh before leaving them hanging there. Aroused and ready, I lift my hips to meet him, my arms braced on the bed. His fingers stroke my buttocks then move between my legs to feel how wet and slick I am for him.

I wait as he positions himself, my body trembling and expectant. He presses his cock into the entrance to my body, rubbing it, stretching it gently before pushing in, so slowly and sweetly that I let out a long moan, almost like a purr. He's so big, so hard, so sweet, and so perfect.

He doesn't move, at first. His hands grip my hips, his fingers gentle but firm on my skin, his cock hot and throbbing inside me. Then he pulls out slowly, almost to the tip, before thrusting in again.

My fingers dig into the sheets, and I press my face onto the soft, fragrant cotton, my moans flowing into the fabric as he fucks me. He takes his time, each thrust angled just right and delivered with the perfect force to make me feel the utmost pleasure. He rolls his hips, aiming for the most sensitive spots, taking my moans as encouragement, his hands palming the soft flesh of my buttocks as every stroke drives me closer to an explosive climax.

My body starts to tighten, surrendering to the pleasure. I hear myself moaning incoherently, all my senses enslaved to the ecstasy, the uncontrollable sweetness spreading from between my legs. I hear

Landon groan, his control starting to unravel as his movements quicken.

"I'm going to come," I hear him say. His voice is rough, ragged. "Oh fuck, Rachel."

I cry out as my body seizes, leaving me momentarily breathless. The pulses of my climax milk him until his own orgasm is over, and afterward, he stretches out on top of me, both of us breathing deeply, our skin misted with sweat.

"I fucking love you," he whispers into my ear.

I breathe into the sheets. "I fucking love you too."

We both doze off for a while, before getting up to prepare for our dinner date. I wear one of the many outfits he got for me, an off-the-shoulder black dress with green accents that match my eyes, and heels in the same color.

I'm standing at the dressing room mirror looking at my reflection when Landon comes behind me to drop a kiss on my neck. I lean my head to the side to give him more space as my eyes meet his in the mirror. Even though I know he's mine, just looking at him still takes my breath away.

He lets his lips trail down to my shoulder, causing a small shiver to pass through me, then he takes my hand and gently fastens a bracelet around my wrist.

I raise my hand to look at the light gold chain, with glittering green stones linked into the metal. “It’s beautiful, Landon.”

“It reminded me of your eyes,” he says.

I turn to face him, my eyes searching his. “You’re spoiling me.”

He takes the hand wearing the bracelet in his. “Do you like it?”

I nod.

“Then that’s all that matters.”

Our reservation is at an intimate restaurant with lovely service and even lovelier food. Landon is smiling and charming, his attention all on me. We talk about everything, and in every second, with every question he asks, every response he gives, with the way his eyes linger on my face, and the way he takes every opportunity to touch me, he makes me feel like the most beautiful woman in the world.

6

After dinner, we return to Landon's apartment, where I fall asleep wrapped up in his arms, and it's the perfect end to a beautiful evening. I sleep peacefully, until his muffled shout jolts me awake a few hours later, and even before I turn on the bedside lamp to see him thrashing, straining, his tortured voice muttering a garbled version of my name, I already know that he's having another nightmare.

I reach for his shoulder, calling his name just as he lets out another pained moan.

"Landon."

His body jerks off the bed, his eyes snapping open,

their expression wild until they focus on me. The look of relief that washes over him is overwhelming to watch.

"Oh God!" his voice is shaky. He reaches for me, taking me into his arms as his chest rises and falls. His skin is damp, even though the room is cool. "You're here."

"Always."

He sighs and pulls me tighter, burying his face in my hair. I put my arms around him, my brow furrowed. What would it take to enable him to move past whatever demons still haunted his dreams? I'd mentioned therapy to him before, and he told me that he'd seen people throughout his teens. Would he consider trying again?

"You're here," he whispers again. Why wouldn't I be? I think back to the last time he'd dreamed of the accident, that last night in San Francisco. He'd dreamed that it was me in the car, that it was me he couldn't save. I'd assumed then, that it had something to do with his fear of hurting me.

Was he still afraid?

I stroke his back while his breathing slows to normal, then he pulls back and gazes deeply into my eyes. "I'm sorry I woke you."

I shake my head, searching his face and trying to read his expression. "How bad was it?"

He shrugs, "It was just a nightmare."

"I know, but… do you want to tell me about it? It seemed pretty rough."

"There's no need," he says, dismissing my concern. "Go back to sleep."

I try to, but I'm worried, especially when I feel him get up soon after, leaving me alone on the bed. When he slips back in, hours later, it's almost dawn. He wakes me with a lingering kiss on my lips, his hands stroking my skin with the particular expertise that soon chases all drowsiness from my mind. Somewhere in the back of my mind is the nagging thought that we should talk about trying to find a solution to his recurrent nightmares, but it soon disappears as I lose myself in the mastery of his touch.

He enters me from behind, his body warm and hard against mine. "I love you," he whispers in my ear, the urgency in his words, in the way he makes love to me, compelling me to put aside any doubts and just trust him.

"I love you," I reply, as pleasure and emotion interweave, leaving me helpless in his arms.

Two intense orgasms later, we share a filling

breakfast in the kitchen. Esmeralda, one of the Swanson Court service staff who works as Landon's housekeeper, brings up and serves our food. She's a plump woman close to middle age, with a sweet face, a permanent smile, and a lilting Eastern European accent. She's obviously fond of Landon and according to him, has been at the Swanson Court for ages.

If Landon is suffering any effects from last night, he doesn't show it. He's the image of the devastatingly sexy CEO in a deep-blue suit, his hair still slightly damp from our shared shower, and brushed back in sleek waves. Looking at him now, it's hard to imagine him any other way but in total control.

"See you in a few hours," he tells me, after the short drive to the Gilt Building. He has just kissed me breathless, and his eyes are burning with intensity, showing me all the things he would do to me as soon as he gets a chance.

"I'll be counting the minutes," I reply, pushing all thoughts of last night from my mind. We'll deal with his nightmares, but maybe not today. For now, I want to enjoy the bliss of knowing that he's mine.

In the office, I'm still working on wiping the love-stoned smile from my face when I get a call from Carole Mendez, Jessica Layner's fire-breathing secretary, summoning me to Jessica's office.

Jessica hasn't asked for me in particular since the day she sent for me and I found Landon waiting in her office. He'd been a stranger then, a stranger I'd slept with. Now, I loved him so much that the magnitude of my emotions made my heart ache.

She is seated at her desk when I walk in, going through some old issues of Gilt Travel, a frown of concentration on her face. She's an older woman, still beautiful, with that ageless quality that money and success often give, when it's not ruined by bad cosmetic work. She looks up when I enter, taking off her glasses to regard me with the frown still on her face.

"Good morning." I shift on my feet, wondering silently what she wants. I have a suspicion that it's about my interview at the Gilt Review. She probably found out somehow. I wonder if she's planning to talk me out of leaving, or to fire me and expedite the process.

"How are you, Rachel?" she asks, motioning for me to sit.

"Fine." I take one of the chairs opposite her and wait, my hands in my lap.

"Are you unhappy here?"

I shake my head. "No."

"Dissatisfied perhaps?"

"No."

She gives me a look. "I'm assuming you know why I'm asking these questions. So you want to move over to the Review?"

"You're aware that I applied to work there initially."

She waves a slim hand dismissively. "Initially. That was what? Two, three years ago?"

"Yes," I pause. "But I still feel that I'm more suited to a place like the Review."

"We discussed this before," she says, "and I told you that there's no such thing as a right fit, especially in a place like Gilt. You have to take ownership of whatever space you find yourself."

I'm not sure if she's selling me some promotional pitch just because she'd rather not lose one of her staff, so I stay silent.

She leans back in her chair and regards me with speculation in her eyes. "Where do you see yourself in say, ten years? Here at Gilt? Doing what?"

"I'd want to be an editor at the Gilt Review," I reply. "Maybe editor in chief."

She smiles. "I thought you might say that. The thing is Rachel. By the time you get to editor in chief, it won't matter which magazine you're working at. You want to work at a literary magazine now, so you're leaving

Travel, but soon, you'll be in a managerial position and the only thing that will matter will be to put out content, sell more magazines and make a profit, whether you're here or at the Review."

I'm not entirely sure she's right, and even if she is, I've wanted this for too long to give it up because of what she thinks. My eyes slip to the pile of magazines on her desk. "When you joined Gilt, which magazine did you want?"

Jessica laughs. "I would have killed to work at Gilt Style. I came in for an interview with my hair perfect, my nails freshly manicured, and somehow they thought I was more suited to making coffee for Tim Bly, he was editor here at the time." She pauses. "You know Gertrude Weyland is taking over at Review, do you?"

I shrug. "I heard."

"I would ask you to wait and see how well she does before throwing in your lot with her, but of course, we know she'll probably do great." She purses her lips. "Mark is leaving soon. You could be a senior editor here before the year runs out. Would you choose that over Review?"

I think about it, and in my mind, I see myself editing travel articles from celebrity writers, thinking up filler pieces and sending features writers off to write promotional articles. I don't want that, but I haven't even gotten the offer from Review yet, and I feel a moment of panic. What if I tell Jessica I don't want Mark's job, and the offer from Gilt Review never materializes?

I shake my head, deciding to trust my heart.

"Very well," Jessica says, putting her glasses back on. "You can go."

I wonder what she'll do. I don't want to underestimate her power within the Gilt family. Could she make it impossible for me to move from Gilt Travel and somehow take away my chance to go to the Review? I have no idea what to expect.

I get up, about to leave, then I stop and face her. "Did you know why Landon Court wanted me to go to San Francisco with him?"

She looks at me from above her glasses, her expression placid. "He never said he wanted you, particularly."

"Of course not," I reply. What had I been thinking? That I would point out that she'd knowingly thrown me into Landon's arms, and she would feel some remorse, and maybe not stand in the way of the job I wanted really badly? She probably thought she'd done me a favor.

I start to walk away, but her voice stops me. "He did seem very interested in you," she says. "I knew his parents, and met him when he was a boy. Apart from a few words at social events, we'd never actually spoken. Suddenly he was offering me an exclusive, and talking about how he'd read your articles. So yes, I could read him from a mile away. There were no conditions, but I was interested. I may be old, but I'm not blind."

"So you decided to send me…to satisfy your curiosity?"

She snorts. "You're overthinking it. I sent you on an official assignment, where you were allowed to conduct yourself in your free time, any way you pleased. So what if Landon Court was attracted to you? That shouldn't have stopped you from being professional, and then if you decided to go the other way and have an adventure. It doesn't make you less of who you are." She frowns at me. "Is that why you want to leave? Because you think I put you in a bad position?

I shake my head. "That's not why I'm leaving."

She sighs. "Because that would be ridiculous. Everyone sometimes has to work with people who find them attractive. It's how you handle it that matters."

How had I handled it? I think of Landon, this morning, his hands on my body, his mouth… I sigh, making an effort to come back to the present.

Jessica is still looking at me, her eyes speculating. She adjusts her glasses. "I hope you'll like it over at Review. I hope you can take advantage of the many opportunities for a young woman like yourself to rise to the top at Gilt." She looks down at the open page on her desk. "You can leave now."

Back in my office, the first email I read on my computer is the offer from the Gilt Review. It's slightly more generous than my current arrangement at Gilt Travel and I quickly call Liz Buckley to accept. Just as we finish the phone call, my door opens and Chelsea comes into my office.

"You won't believe what I just heard," she exclaims. "Jack Weyland is leaving Gilt."

So he was really leaving. I'm surprised and pleased by how little the knowledge affects me. "Yeah, I know."

Chelsea gives me a look. "How come? Everyone else is just finding out."

"He told me last week," I say. "Stalked me on my way to lunch."

"Awww." She pauses. "I saw him hurrying out after

you that night at Insomnia. What happened?"

"He was being a total asshole about Landon," I grimace. "He said he loves me," I roll my eyes. "Imagine that."

"I thought it might be something like that," she mutters. "Men are crazy. First they want you, then they don't, then as soon as it seems like they can't get you, they just can't let you go."

I arch a brow at her. "Wanna tell me about it? Is it the hot neighbor?"

She sighs. "He's driving me crazy, but I'll tell you another time. I'm trying not to dwell on my feelings."

I nod, totally getting it. "I have news too. I'm also leaving Gilt Travel."

She looks dismayed. "No!"

"Yes." My smile widens. "I'm moving to Review."

Chelsea squeals and comes around the desk to hug me. "I hate you so much right now, but I'm so happy for you. Does that make sense?"

"It does."

She makes a sad face. "My workload is going to fucking skyrocket. I fucking hate you. How am I going to finish my book?"

I stick out my tongue. "I'll read and edit for you anytime you're ready. I'm an assistant editor at The Gilt

Review now. It's obvious that I know literature."

After she leaves, I reach for my phone, eager to call Landon and tell him my news. I'm almost deliriously happy. I have my dream job, the man I love… It's as if everything I've ever wanted has finally come to me.

The thought comes with a little sliver of fear, especially when my mind goes back to last night. How long can I expect things to stay perfect? How long until something comes along to ruin it?

I shake the fear away and make the call to Landon. He answers on the first ring, almost as if he'd been waiting for me.

"Rachel." His voice is deep, warm, and sexy.

"Hi," I breathe.

"What's going on?"

I sigh, so lost in his voice that I have to try to remember why I called in the first place. "I...um… I got the job."

"I knew you would." He sounds very confident.

"Really?"

"Yes, because they have to know how lucky they'd be to have you."

"Aww." His faith in me is so gratifying. I spend the next few minutes telling him about the meeting with Jessica, leaving out the part where we talked about him.

"It sounds like she didn't want to lose you."

"Oh well." I shrug.

"So," he pauses. "Did you ever solve the mystery of how you got the interview?"

"Oh… I'm not quite sure, but…" I tell him about the dinner with Gertrude Weyland, and Jack's belief that she had something to do with it.

Landon is quiet, and for a moment, I wonder if he's thinking of the part about me going with Jack to visit his mother, or having lunch with him.

"Are you sure you want to work with her?" he says finally. He sounds more concerned than jealous.

"I don't mind," I reply. "She seemed interesting."

"You could try to confirm if she had anything to do with it. Find out what she wants, and if you don't like it, you can always take me up on my offer and come work for me."

"Nice try." I smile. "What exactly would I do at Swanson Court International?"

"Anything you want. You could be my boss if you like. You already are, in a way."

"If I were your boss, you wouldn't be on the phone with your girlfriend."

"You see why we need you around here?" His voice is half-serious.

"Stop trying to steal me away from my job." I chuckle. There were enough people saying goodbye to Gilt already. "Jack is leaving Gilt too," I mention.

There is a short pause. "I know."

"How?" I frown. "People in my office only found out today."

He sighs. "I happen to own a small stake in a production company that just signed a very lucrative deal with him."

A few alarm bells go off in my head. "So you have something to do with him leaving?"

"I had nothing to do with the deal," Landon explains. "I only have the information because I'm a shareholder." His voice turns serious. "I'm not insecure about us Rachel, and I trust you. Although, it's flattering that you think I'm powerful enough to press a button and send Jack Weyland across the country just because I don't want him around you."

I breathe, glad to be wrong. "I'm not sorry he's leaving," I say. "It's just... it's great that you don't think that I'm still attracted to him or anything like that."

"I don't." His voice is firm. "Forget Weyland. The most important right now is that we have to celebrate your new job. What would you like to do?"

"Why don't you think of something?" What I don't

say is that being with him is already celebration enough for me.

"I will," Landon promises. "See you tonight, baby."

"See you tonight, beau."

His laughter teases my ears as I go back to work, and I don't even bother to try to wipe the smile off my face.

We celebrate with a candlelit dinner at Landon's apartment, and afterward we make love, both of us flush with good food and wine, then he takes me home so I can help Laurie with her packing.

The rest of the week follows the same pattern, dinner at his place, and making love in his bed before he takes me home to my apartment.

Before I can really get used to the fact that Laurie is actually moving out, Saturday arrives. Brett comes over to help with the lifting. Landon comes too, joining Brett in carrying the heavier boxes while Laurie and I make a big deal out of encouraging them and admiring their muscles.

Brett has a truck waiting downstairs. The driver, Malik, is an acquaintance from the gym, and with his help, it doesn't take long to get Laurie's things into the back of the truck.

When we're done, we all stand outside on the sidewalk, me and Laurie hugging over and over again while Malik drives off. A taxi is already waiting to take her and Brett to their new apartment.

"Are you sure you won't need help over there," Landon asks Brett, The long sleeves of his gray t-shirt are rolled up and the wind is ruffling his hair. He looks manly and sexy and I can't wait to get him back inside so I can pounce on him. "We could come."

Brett shakes his head. "There really isn't much. I'm sure Malik and I can manage." He looks at me and winks, "I know you can't wait for us to leave you two alone."

I snort. "Don't tease me, Brett. Not when I still hate you for stealing my cousin away."

"I'm not taking her to Siberia," he exclaims. "You can still see each other every day if you want."

"You won't understand," Laurie tells him. "We're obligatory twins."

Landon chuckles. "There's no such thing."

"Of course there is," I reply, starting to explain. "It's when your parents are twins, but you're not. You're cousins but obligated to be twins."

"Like us," Laurie agrees, "and the obligation grows

on you until you can't imagine life without it."

Both Landon and Brett look at us as if we're crazy, then they shake hands in that casual but charming guy way. "Thanks, bro," Brett tells him, before turning to Laurie. "My lady, your chariot awaits."

She sticks out her tongue in a very unladylike manner, before hugging me one more time, and then they're gone. Upstairs, the apartment feels unbelievably empty. Almost everything is the same, because Laurie didn't take much, but I feel her absence nonetheless.

"It feels so empty!" I complain.

Landon closes the door behind him and comes to slide his strong arms around my waist, nuzzling my neck with his warm, firm lips. "Empty serves my purpose at the moment," he murmurs. "And, as Brett said, you can see Laurie as often as you want. She's not that far away."

I arch my neck, giving him more space to trail kisses along my skin. "It won't be the same though."

His lips move from my neck to my shoulder, and my breath hitches as the first waves of desire fan out of my belly. "Maybe I could console you?"

I turn around to face him, a smile playing on my lips. "All words," I tease, "no action."

A single eyebrow goes up, and he grins, a predatory look crossing his features as he lifts me off my feet. I wrap my legs around his waist, my arms around his neck as he carries me into my bedroom. He sets me down on the bed and covers my body with his. "This kind of action, you mean?"

I shrug, looking up into his eyes. "Maybe."

His laugh is soft as he lowers his head and covers my lips with his, his tongue gently pushing into my mouth.

I moan, my fingers digging into his hair as his lips move over mine, his tongue teasing and caressing mine while he grinds his body against me, making me aware of his need for me. I kiss him back, breathless with desire, grateful when he works magic with my clothes, making them disappear. Soon I'm naked beneath him, but he's still fully dressed.

"It's not fair that you have so many clothes on," I complain breathlessly. I push my hands under his t-shirt, my fingers running over his rock hard abs. "I want you naked."

Landon laughs. "Be patient." His words are followed by another long kiss, which leaves me trembling, aching, and needy. After he has thoroughly plundered my mouth, he starts on a sweet trail from my lips to my neck, and down to my breasts. He gives one nipple a slow sensuous lave with his tongue, then he does the same with the other breast, licking both nipples until they're pebbled and sensitive under his tongue. When I'm moaning helplessly, my body writhing with pleasure, he gets to his feet and pulls his t-shirt over his head.

I feast my eyes on his perfection, sighing helplessly, lustfully. He tosses the t-shirt and holds my gaze for a silent moment.

"Are you going to do a striptease?" I ask, eager for him, but sure that I can control my lust for long enough to watch him work his body.

He reaches for his belt, a smile curving his lips. "I want you to think of me as sexy, not as the comic relief."

"Live a little," I encourage, winking at him. "Show me those Landon Court moves."

"Landon Court moves?" He's grinning as he pulls off his pants, then his briefs, revealing his turgid, drool-worthy erection. My lips part with hunger and anticipation. I watch as he advances toward the bed. "Don't worry," he tells me, eyes smoky. "I'll show you."

I lick my lips, lifting my face for a kiss as he stretches his body over mine. I spread my legs for him, kissing him back and at the same time guiding him to where I need him the most. He lingers at the entrance, the head of his cock rubbing my slick flesh, then with a long sigh he pushes deep inside, filling me completely.

There is a surge of heat, so sweet, so ineffably beautiful. I hold on to him, feeling his muscles tense and tighten as he moves his hips, each slow stroke more delicious than the one that came before.

I hold on to his gaze, seeing my arousal mirrored in his eyes. My lips move, forming his name as sensations overwhelm me, until it feels as if I'm going to drown in them. I surrender myself to him, the first wave of my climax rolling over me and making me cry out. Landon continues to move, increasing my pleasure with every deep thrust. By the time he finally loses control and comes with a loud groan, I'm exhausted and limp with fulfilled desire.

"You're so beautiful," he says later, when I'm lying naked in his arms. "I'm never letting you go."

I press my body closer to his. "I'm not going anywhere."

7

We spend the rest of the day in bed, only getting out to order food before having a playful dinner in front of the TV. I fall asleep with my head in Landon's lap, his fingers gently stroking my hair. Later, I wake up long enough to bury my face in his hair as he carries me to my bed, undressing us both and laying behind me, his hard body flush against my back.

"I love you," I whisper sleepily.

I feel his lips on the nape of my neck. "And I love you."

I wake up sometime during the night to find myself alone on the bed. Landon is not in the room or in the bathroom, and for a single moment of panic, I wonder if he has gone back to his apartment, and why. I find him in the living room, watching something on the TV with the volume turned off. Sighing in relief, I join him on the couch, one hand curving around his. I know that at least a part of the reason he's not sleeping is because he's avoiding his nightmares.

"Hey," I whisper.

"Hey." He smiles at me. "You should be asleep."

"So should you." I shrug. "I decided I wanted to watch… whatever it is you're watching."

Landon chuckles, pulling me into his side and dropping a soft kiss on my temple. We spend the rest of the night watching some of Laurie's shows and laughing our heads off. I finally doze off when it starts to get light outside, and when I wake up a few hours later, Landon is leaning back on the couch, asleep, with a peaceful expression on his face.

I spend a long moment looking at his face, overcome by the depth of my emotions. I love him more than I have the capacity to put into words. He's my soulmate, the only one I could ever love like this, and I know I would give anything to be with him always, to be this happy always.

Careful not to wake him, I get up and go to the kitchen to make coffee and try to rustle up a passable breakfast. By the time I'm done, Landon is awake, his hair still damp from a shower in my bathroom. He's wearing his pants from yesterday, but his chest is bare, the well-defined muscles more perfectly sculpted than any male model's.

"Good morning," I whistle suggestively, wondering at how his tall frame dwarfs the entire kitchen.

"Good morning." He gives me a slow, sexy smile that makes my insides melt. "Can I help?"

I shake my head. "I'm kinda done."

He comes behind me and covers my back with his body. I sigh and lean into him, enjoying his touch, and so happy because he is mine to touch.

"I can't begin to explain how grateful I am for you, how…" he breathes, "How happy you make me."

I turn around and face him, aware that my eyes are misting. There is an intensity in his cobalt gaze that reaches into my heart, squeezing until I feel like I'm drowning in emotion. I don't know how to reply, so I stay silent.

"When I'm with you I feel complete." He chuckles softly. "I never thought I'd say that to anyone. I've never felt that I needed anyone to be complete, but being without you would kill me."

"You're never going to be without me," I tell him

softly. Nothing would ever make me stop loving him, and I'm determined that nothing would ever make me walk away from him again.

I remain in his arms, resting my head on his chest. "I want to stop time," I whisper. "So we'll always be like this."

He pulls back, his eyes on mine. "Are you afraid that things might change in future?"

I sigh. "I don't know."

"We'll always be like this," he assures me, pulling me back into his arms. "Older, after a while, but there'll never be anything else for me like what we have."

I let out a shaky breath. "I love you."

"Well, I'm irresistible," he says with a playful smirk. "You didn't stand a chance."

I smack him playfully, laughing as he picks up the plates and carries them to the living room. We settle on the floor in front of the couch, eating while we continue our TV binge.

"Have you thought of what you'll do about the apartment?" Landon asks after. He's sitting on the couch, and I'm on the floor between his legs, trying not to drift off as he plays with my hair.

"I'll probably find a roommate." I make a face. "I can't imagine living with anyone but Laurie."

There is a short pause as his fingers still in my hair. "Even me?"

For a moment, I'm not sure I heard right. I turn around to face him. "You?"

His eyes stay on mine. "Why not?"

I look down from his gaze, not sure why I'm hesitating. I would love to go to sleep and wake up in his arms every night, and I know what a leap it is for him, how much it means that he's inviting me to share his life so completely.

I wish I weren't so afraid that something would go wrong, especially if we move too fast and shake the balance we've already found. "I don't know..." I reply softly.

Landon is looking at me, as if he's waiting for me to say more. "It seems like a good solution to me," he says, when I stay silent. "My apartment is closer to your office and we'd be able to spend more time together."

And I want that, to spend more time with him. He's right, of course. He has obviously thought about this, but I haven't… I need to think, to be sure that we don't rush, that we don't get overconfident, and ruin what we have, because if that happens... I'm not sure that I'll survive.

"Think about it," Landon says quietly, urging me

back to my former position. His hands resume their ministrations in my hair. "And while you're doing that, maybe you'd like to spend this week with me."

"As a foretaste?" I say lightly.

I can almost feel his grin. "What else?"

"You don't have to try to convince me," I say sincerely. "I want to move in with you. I just want a little time to think about it."

"I'm not trying…" He stops. "Well, maybe I am trying to get you comfortable with the idea, but more than that, I want you, with me, every night for the next few days, because I have plans for you."

My breath hitches at his sensual tone, after a week of having to leave him almost every night, I'm more than ready for one where I spend the whole night in his arms. "Of course, I'll spend the week with you."

Later, Landon watches while I get ready to leave with him. I don't have to take much, because thanks to him, I have a closet in his house with everything I need.

I toss my ereader in my bag and turn to face him. "I guess that's it," I say, rolling my eyes. "Some guy I know bought me a whole wardrobe at his apartment."

"He seems generous." Landon rises from the bed to help me put on a jacket over my sleeveless dress. Over his t-shirt, he's wearing the dark jacket he brought with him yesterday. "You should reward him."

I turn around and run a finger down his chest. "With what?"

He gives me a naughty grin. "Sex always works."

"Ah," I smile back. "That wouldn't be fair to him." My smile widens as Landon's eyebrow goes up. "Sex with him is as much a reward for me as it is for him."

"You're too good for my ego." His gaze turns serious and he takes my face in his hands. "I could spend the rest of my life trying to tell you all the different ways I'm in love with you, and it wouldn't be enough. If I make you feel even a quarter of the things you make me feel. I'd die a happy man."

I close my eyes, letting the words wash over me. I open them to find him still looking at me. I breathe softly. "Landon… I can't explain…the way you make me feel…" I give him a helpless look. "Sometimes 'I love you' seems so trite."

He lowers his head and brushes his lips over mine. I hold on, craving his touch. After a few seconds, he releases me, and I reach for my bag, my legs unsteady. "You're not dying anytime soon," I say lightly. "Happy or otherwise."

"Okay, ma'am." Grinning, he takes the bag from me and leans in to whisper in my ear. "I'm going to make love to you again, but if I don't have lunch before I do, dying happy won't be so far-fetched."

Downstairs, Landon's car, the one he came with yesterday, is parked in one of the spaces in front of my building. It's one I haven't seen before, a black sports car with bucket seats in soft cream leather and an engine that purrs like a kitten.

Our destination is a bustling Italian restaurant where the manager, an older woman with red hair and humorous eyes, greets Landon with the familiarity of a regular. "Welcome, Mr. Court," she exclaims, her eyes flicking from him to me with thinly veiled interest.

Landon shakes his head. "It's Landon to you, Angela."

"Actually, it's little Landon, but I choose not to call you that in front of your girlfriend."

Landon laughs, and she gives him a strange look, almost as if his good mood has taken her by surprise. She holds out a hand to me. "I'm Angela. I used to work at the Swanson Court in the old days."

In the old days. I wonder if that's before or after Landon's mother died. I take her hand. "Rachel

Foster."

"I know." Her eyes are shining as she smiles at me. "I catch a few gossip items in the news every now and then."

"Oh." I look over at Landon, but he only shrugs, his eyes full of amusement. We follow Angela to a secluded table, and she personally supervises the waiter that serves our food, which, of course, is delicious.

"How's the food?" Landon asks.

"Do you need to ask?" I sigh. "It's wonderful. You obviously know where all the good food is in this city. If I keep eating like this, I'll need to take Brett up on his offer of free membership at the gym."

"There's a gym at the apartment, you could use that."

I give him a look. "If you're trying to make your apartment more attractive to me, please refrain from mentioning the gym."

He grins. "I am trying to make it more attractive to you."

"As long as it has you in it, it's already the most attractive it can possibly be."

An eyebrow goes up, but he only smiles and continues to eat. I know he'll respect my need for more time to think about living with him, so I concentrate on enjoying the rest of my food.

Angela soon returns to the table to fuss. "Enjoying your meal?"

I nod. "It's wonderful, thank you."

"I taught your boyfriend here to make pasta sauce like no other," She informs me.

I look at Landon and he confirms it with a nod. "True."

"You haven't made her that yet?" She gives him a reproachful glare. "What are you waiting for?"

Landon leans back on his chair and moves his shoulders in a small shrug. "I'm biding my time, waiting for the right moment to seal the deal with my perfect pasta sauce." He looks at me and grins. "It'll ruin you for every other man."

You've already ruined me for every other man, I want to tell him, but I turn to Angela instead. "He's always been this confident?" I ask, knowing that the answer is probably yes. "You'd have to make it now," I tell Landon, "so I can decide if it's really as good as you claim."

"She only loves me for my cooking," Landon tells Angela, laughing. "Who would have thought?"

The older woman is looking at me. "Amongst other things, I'm sure." She gives me a strange smile, blinking rapidly, and I wonder if she's getting emotional. When we're done with the meal, she follows us outside and surprises me by giving me a hug. "It was nice to meet you, Rachel," she says, adding in a small whisper. "Thank you for making him so happy."

I watch her walk back inside, then allow Landon to take my hand as we emerge onto the sidewalk. "She seems very fond of you."

"Yes," he agrees. "I'm fond of her too. I was lucky in a way, growing up the way I did. I was surrounded by a couple of wonderful people, most of whom I still have in my life."

He starts to lead me along the sidewalk, and I'm so comfortable walking arm in arm that it takes me a few minutes to remember that we drove over. "What about the car?"

Landon pulls me closer, so his arm is around me. "I arranged for someone to get it. It's not a long walk."

"I know." I lean into his body as we meander along the sidewalk. I love how ordinary it feels, just another couple out on a Sunday afternoon. He buys me a bunch of flowers from a street vendor, and I blush with pleasure when he hands them to me. We take our time, his arm around my shoulder and mine around his waist. I breathe in his scent, loving the warmth from his body and the feel of his t-shirt against my fingers. I turn my face up to look at his, and his eyes meet mine, blue and beautiful. The wind touches his hair, ruffling his beautiful waves and I reach out to smooth them. How did one person get to be so perfect? I wonder with a soft sigh.

Landon gives me an anxious glance. "Are you cold?"

"No," I shake my head. It's windy, and there's a small bite in the air, but I love it. I love the fact that the seasons are changing, that I'm with him, right here, right now.

He raises a brow. "Because you can't be cold when I'm right here to warm you up."

"You have a one-track mind."

"Who said anything about sex?"

"Now you have."

He laughs. "I have it on good authority that you find my performance very rewarding."

I shake my head, unable to stop my laughter. "You're a sex fiend."

"A sexy one, you mean?" He's laughing. "You're my weakness, you know, and my strength. My everything."

We stop walking as he leans in to kiss me properly. His lips are firm but sweet and caressing, and when he stops, I release a breath and open my eyes. There's a silly smile on my face as I look up at him.

"What?" he says. "Have I stolen your voice with my superb kissing skills?"

I'm about to retort when someone calls out. "Give us another one, Court!"

We both turn in the direction of the voice. The photographer is a skinny guy with sharp eyes, wearing a hoodie and sweats. He grins at us and gives Landon a thumbs-up. Landon frowns and turns to me. "Come on," he says. We're very close to the Swanson Court now, which explained the presence of the photographer. With the scattering of luxury hotels in the area, there were always a few of them waiting to catch a glimpse of celebrities, and to many people, a young, sexy, wealthy man like Landon was as interesting as the usual crop of Hollywood stars.

"Do you mind?" Landon asks softly. "It'll probably get published in some gossip column or the other."

I shrug. "Of course not. I'll probably have to get used to it since they find you so interesting." I peer at his face. "Do you mind?"

He laughs. "No. I want the whole world to know that you belong to me."

I breathe, closing my eyes as his hand goes around my shoulder again, and we continue to walk. My arm finds its way around his waist, my fingers resting lightly on his body through the thin barrier of his t-shirt. My heart is aching sweetly with an almost unbearable happiness, and in that moment, I love him a thousand times more than I ever thought it was possible to love anyone.

We spend the rest of the day at his apartment. Landon gives me what he laughingly calls the premier girlfriend tour of the whole apartment. It's actually much larger than I first thought. Downstairs, there's his study, the fully-equipped gym, the library, den, dining room and kitchen, and upstairs, more bedrooms, another sitting room, and a couple of empty rooms. One of them used to be the nursery and playroom, he tells me, and the other, a spacious room with large windows, a few empty bookshelves and a beautiful view of the park, used to be his mother's sitting room.

"We moved most of the stuff to the house after the accident," Landon says, explaining why the room is empty.

I take a moment to admire the spectacular view from the windows. "It must have been a lovely room."

"It was." He smiles softly and takes the hand I offer him, leading me back downstairs to his study. It's smaller than his office at the SCT building, but with the daunting view and large desk, it gives the same impression of power.

"What is it with men and large desks," I ask teasingly, running a hand over the polished wood. I prop myself on the surface and notice the picture I gave him, the racier one, sitting right next to the large computer screen. "So this is what you stare at when you're supposed to be making money?"

"I can't help myself." He laughs, coming to sit on his high-backed swivel chair and drawing it closer to the edge of the desk so he's right in front of me. "I get hard whenever I look at it."

I wet my lips as his hands glide under my dress and over my thighs, drawing slowly toward the edge of my panties. His touch is searing, starting a fire that burns into my skin, through my blood, and right to my core. "Spread your legs for me, baby," Landon whispers.

I do as he says, leaning my elbows on the polished surface of the desk, my eyes on his. He moves his hand between my thighs, his teasing fingers finding me through my light cotton panties. I throw my head back, sighing as he strokes me gently, rubbing my clit with the pad of his thumb.

"You like that?" His voice is husky.

"Hmmm… yes."

I hear him chuckle and the next moment he's hooking a finger into the crotch of my panties and pushing them out of the way. Then his tongue is on me - light and sweet - licking, sucking, stroking, and driving me wild with pleasure.

I fall back on the desk, my hips writhing, my fingers finding his hair and pulling on the silky strands. He kicks the chair back, getting on his knees with his head still buried between my thighs. He licks my clit with sweet, gentle strokes, the tip of his tongue nudging the tiny bud before moving lower, over my folds, to my already pulsing entrance. He plunges his tongue deep inside me, and all my muscles turn to hot, molten desire.

Soon, my hips are bucking, rolling, and my whole body twisting with almost unbearable pleasure. I can feel his tongue, his fingers, the beginning of an orgasm building at my core, with heat spreading until all my lower body is a pulsing center of intense pleasure.

I draw up my legs when I come, my whole body rearing off the desk as if I'm having a seizure. Landon grips my thighs, his tongue continuing to torture me with pleasure until I beg him to stop. He raises his head, smiling at my heavy lidded and languid expression before he rises to his feet and moves the chair back toward the desk. He shifts to the very edge, pulling me off the desk to straddle his thighs.

I'm still feeling dazed from my orgasm, and I have to place my hands on his shoulders for balance. I wait while he undoes his pants, just enough so he can free the stiff column of his cock, then he lifts me by my hips, one hand holding my panties aside while he gently guides me down, until his whole length is sheathed inside me.

The pleasurable feeling of fullness brings me to life. A low sound escapes me, almost like a purr. The tips of my toes are touching the carpeted floor, only barely, but enough for me to put my weight on them while I lift my body, then push back down, riding him as hard as I want, as hard as I need.

There's something incredibly erotic about the fact that we're both fully dressed. His hands mold my thighs and buttocks under my dress, kneading my flesh almost feverishly. His teeth find a nipple through the material of my dress and bra, and the feeling makes me want to tear off my clothes to give him more access, yet I can't stop riding him for long enough to do that, the pleasure is too much, too intense.

Arching my back, I take him deeper, so I can feel his balls, warm against my sensitive skin. I ride him faster, almost frantically, practically senseless against everything but how good he feels, how much I want him…

My eyes are closed, but I hear his loud groan as he rises from the chair, taking me with him. My legs wrap around his waist, my arms tight around his shoulders as he keeps me up with his strong arms, ramming forcefully into me, his breaths coming in low grunts. He lowers me to the desk, and I feel the polished wood against my buttocks, and Landon, thrusting, hard, deep, relentlessly. I let go of his shoulders, my body falling back on the desk, my arms tightening around my breasts as another orgasm builds and rips right through me.

I think I black out for a moment. When I come to my senses, Landon's body is curved over mine, shuddering with the force of his own climax.

"I'm not sure I'll be able to get any work done on this desk ever again," he tells me, a dazed expression on his face.

I know the look is mirrored on mine. Sex has never felt this good with anyone before. It has never felt this complete, this pleasurable, or this fulfilling, and I know it never will, not with anyone but him.

8

"I'm so glad you're still going to be in the building," Chelsea says as we head out of my final meeting with the features team.

"Me too," I'm feeling a little emotional. I handed in my notice first thing in the morning, and during the meeting with the other writers, Mark announced to everyone that I was leaving Gilt Travel. I'm still reeling from all the hugs and love I'd received afterward.

Reading my mood, Chelsea leaves me at the door to my office and I'm grateful for the solitude. There's always something poignant about making a change in one's life, I decide. Even though the change was something I wanted, I still felt a little raw inside.

Of course, the biggest change was something I hadn't even allowed myself to think about. Moving in with Landon.

I want to. God knows I want to, with all my heart.

And he loves me. I don't doubt that he does.

So why am I hesitating?

My phone rings, interrupting my thoughts. Glancing down at the screen, I smile when I see Laurie's name.

"Yeah?" I answer pointedly. "New phone, who dis?"

Laurie starts to laugh. "Shut up."

"You abandoned me for a man," I accuse. "You are not forgiven."

"I know I am." She sounds confident, as if she knows I can't be angry with her for any extended period. "You can't hold out for this long."

"How are you?" I ask softly, suddenly missing her.

She sighs. "Happy. What about you?"

"Landon asked me to move in with him."

Laurie whistles. "You know, I was kinda expecting that. I think I saw it in his eyes on Saturday. But then, he always looks like he can't wait to just… eat you up," she laughs. "So what did you tell him?"

"Nothing," I close my eyes, imagining what she'll

say. "I'm still thinking about it."

"Knowing you, that probably means you're thinking of reasons not to." I can almost see her eye roll. "What's there to think about, Rachel? He loves you. You love him."

"Yeah, but…" I search for the right words to explain my hesitation. "Moving in together is such a big step. Are we ready for that? A few weeks ago, I was sure we were over. How many couples actually grow closer after they start living together? What if… you know, we get used to each other and become bored, then fall out of love."

Laurie snorts. "Now you're being ridiculous."

"I am aren't I?" I sigh. "I just… I have this fear. I love him so much. If anything went wrong. I'd..."

"Nothing will go wrong!" she exclaims. "Rach, there's so much that's only in your head. What's the worst that can happen? Live a little! I, for one, believe that Landon would rather cut off a part of his anatomy than hurt you."

That makes me smile. "Which part?"

Laurie cackles. "And I'm the one with the dirty mind?" She laughs some more, then continues. "Rach, say yes to that poor guy. I believe he suffers when you're not in his line of sight."

I chuckle. "Okay."

"That probably means you'll keep thinking and thinking yourself out of it." I hear her snort. "Anyway, why I really called. I sent a link to your office email. Take a look."

I navigate to my inbox on my computer and find the link. It's an article with the picture of Landon and me kissing on the sidewalk. It's actually a lovely picture, and the website is a reputable news site, not one of the tabloids where I'd expected it to end up.

The accompanying article is also very tasteful. "Hotelier Landon Court spotted with his girlfriend, Rachel Foster. Court's reps confirm that the two have been together for a couple of months. Miss Foster is an editor at Gilt publications, and her parents are renowned painter Lynne Foster, and Trent Foster of the high street clothing line Trent & Taylor.

Pictures from some of the events we've attended together also accompany the article, among them the champagne mixer and the Gold Dust opening in San Francisco.

"Cool, right?" Laurie says in a dreamy voice. "You look so pretty and in love."

"Yeah," I whisper, remembering the kiss, and thinking that somehow Landon must have taken control of the situation with the tabloid photographer. He probably bought the pictures and engaged a reputable journalist to put out the story the way he wanted.

"I'm going to have to get used to seeing you in the news," Laurie is saying. "And you have to make sure you always look on point. You never know when someone is going to take a picture."

I snort, imagining a life of always being under some sort of spotlight. "I'd rather not think about it. Let's talk about Barbados instead."

Laurie's compromise with her mother was that if she agreed to go all the way to Barbados, then the wedding would take place as soon as possible. The date they'd set was only weeks away, and I thought it was perfect, mainly because I'm not very fond of drawn-out periods of event planning. I also think it's lucky how our parents seem to find the opportunity to plan a wedding as an exciting interruption to their retirement, or semi-retirement in my mother's case. They've taken over most of the arrangements and the planning, and Laurie with her busy schedule doesn't really mind. In fact, she loves it.

"I'm sending you all the appointments for the following two weeks," she tells me now. "My dress, your dress… Mom found me this stylist, and she wants to do a test run, so we'll go get our makeup and hair done, so that for the two of us at least, she'll know what she'll be working with on the day of the wedding."

"Sounds great," I reply, looking forward to the time I'll be spending with her. After a few more minutes on the phone, she has to get back to work, and I start the task of cleaning up my desk, doing all my pending work, and writing my handover notes. I'm not even close to done by the end of the day. When Landon calls, I'm so relieved to have an excuse to stop.

"Hey,"

"Hello, sugar."

"Hmmm," I grin, "I like that."

"The endearment?" His voice is soft. "I have many more where that came from."

"I'm looking forward to hearing them."

"You will," he promises. "What are you doing this weekend?"

I only think a moment before I reply. "You?"

Landon laughs. "Now that we've cleared that up,

how would you like to do 'me' somewhere far away?"

I loved all the trips I've taken with him. He has the same love of quiet, serene places that I do. "Where do you have in mind?"

"You'll see." His voice gives nothing away and I have to stem my curiosity.

"You just love this weekend jaunts, don't you?"

"I have a beautiful girlfriend to impress."

"I'm already very, very impressed."

"Allow me to keep blowing your mind, my darling." When my only response is a soft sigh of pleasure, he continues. "So, what do you say?"

"Hmm," I pretend to think about it. "Let me see… Do I want to spend the weekend with my sexy boyfriend?" I hear him chuckle. "Of course I'll come."

"Thank you, gorgeous. You've given me something to look forward to for the rest of the week."

"I'm glad," I reply, delighted as well. Remembering the article from this morning, I continue. "Laurie sent me the link to an article about us with the picture from yesterday. It was really tasteful, and they quoted your people."

"Yes, that." There's a short pause from him. "There's always going to be a story," he says finally. "I took control of this one. I want the world to know about us, but I'd rather they heard from me, and not some pseudo-reporter in a sleazy tabloid."

"You're so anal," I tease, but I understand why he would do what he did. It made our relationship seem less casual, less like a rumor, when his own reps had contributed to the article.

"I am thorough." Landon corrects smugly. "There's a difference."

"Anal," I insist.

He laughs. "How are your colleagues taking your move?"

"They're all weeping inconsolably at their desks begging me not to go."

"Lucky you. Over here, if I told them I was leaving… Going to start a colony in outer space or something, they'll probably light a bonfire and dance around it all night."

"Somehow, I don't think that's true," I reply, sure that if I am lucky, it's because I have him. "I think they may be planning to throw me a party over here, which is good, but they're making me prepare my handover notes. It's taken all day and I'm famished."

"Haven't you had lunch?"

I shake my head. "Would you believe if I tell you that I forgot?"

"Let's have an early dinner then." His voice is laced with concern, which makes me smile. "I could pick you up in a few."

I'm trying to identify the emotion coursing through me, and I realize it's that feeling of delight arising from being cared for by someone I love. I love it. I really do. I close my eyes. "Yes please."

We have dinner at Mancini, and Landon is his teasing, attentive and sexy self, watching me indulgently as I wolf down my food.

"Aidan's play is opening next week Thursday," he informs me. "You'll come, won't you?"

"As if anything would keep me away."

"Ha!" He laughs. "I have to be careful with you around him, so he doesn't steal you from me."

I dab my lips with a napkin. "I'm not a possession to be stolen or owned, Mr. Court," I say in my best Lauren Bacall impression.

He raises one perfect brow and my mind is

momentarily derailed with thoughts of how amazingly gorgeous he is, and how lucky I am. "Don't I know that? You own me, however, and I'm glad to be your possession." He looks so serious that I can't resist the smile that pulls at my lips.

"You're so cute when you're charming."

"No," he replies. "I'm charming when I'm charming."

"Oh!" I raise my brows. "Is that what the women tell you?"

"What women?" He grins. "There's only one woman. There's only ever been one woman." He reaches out and touches the edge of my lip. "And she's right here."

Lord! "I love you, Landon."

He doesn't reply immediately. His eyes scour my face, blue and dazzling, blazing with emotion. When he finally speaks, his voice is soft and clearly communicates the depth of his feelings for me. "There is absolutely nothing about you that doesn't make me feel like I'm the luckiest man in the world."

I sigh, my heart floating to an unexplored plane of pure pleasure. "You're killing me here."

His grin tells me that he's aware of the effect his

words have on me. "The Hayes are coming to town for Aidan's opening night. You remember Wilson and Betsy?"

"Of course." Wilson Hayes was the former manager of the Swanson Court New York, who was now retired and managing Windbreakers, Landon's home upstate. He'd been the main father figure in Landon's life, at least after his mother died. "I'd like to see them."

He pours me some more wine. "They'd love to see you," he says. "Dinner then, on Friday next week? The day after the play."

I nod. "Okay."

Landon's eyes wander from my face, down the front of my dress. "Now that I've bought you dinner," he says with a naughty grin, "Can we leave so I can put your new found energy to good use?"

"I think I'll linger for a while," I tease, pretending that I'm not as eager to devour him as he is for me. "I love the ambiance of this place."

He looks around the dimly lit restaurant. "Fuck the ambiance," he mutters, turning back to me and letting the smolder his eyes communicate exactly what he wants to do to me. "I need to be inside you."

I bite the corner of my lip. "Okay, boyfriend," I

reply, forcing a lightness into my voice that belies the pleasant ache of arousal building in my lower belly, “When you put it like that, how can I resist?”

9

The next day, I have one of my final interviews at a travel app startup that has gotten widely popular in the last few months. The office is close to Landon's building, so when I'm done, I decide to surprise him.

At the gleaming marble lobby of the SCT building, the security personnel wave me through to the elevators, but on Landon's floor, the receptionist gives me a strange glance as she buzzes open the glass security doors. She greets me with a smile before she quickly picks up the phone.

Deciding not to wonder if surprising Landon was such a good idea, I continue to his office. At the large outer office, Tony Gillies isn't there to greet me, but one of the other assistants meet me at the door.

"Hello Miss Foster, I'm Sharon." She's about my age, smiling, but brisk in her manner. "Mr. Court is in a meeting now."

"Okay." I glance at my watch. "I'll wait."

She starts to say something else, but at that moment the opaque glass doors to Landon's office open and Ava Sinclair walks out.

I suddenly can't hear what Sharon is saying. My eyes are locked on Landon, who's holding the door open for Ava. He doesn't see me at first, he's too busy saying goodbye to Ava, the fond smile on his face making my stomach tense.

After a final word of goodbye, Ava starts to walk toward the exit, toward me. Her eyes flick over me, and her lips lift in her signature smirk, then as she walks past me, she winks.

I turn back to Landon, and he's looking at me with a mixture of surprise and pleasure, and something else too. Apprehension maybe. I swallow the annoyance on the tip of my tongue, the jealousy boiling in my stomach, and the questions. What was she doing here? And that hateful, mocking wink? If I never saw that woman ever again, it would be too soon.

Landon is walking toward me now, and I try not to

get distracted by how immaculate he looks in his suit, how perfectly the waves of his hair frame his heartbreakingly beautiful face. He reaches where I'm standing and drops a kiss to my mouth, and once he's standing so close, and I'm surrounded by *him*, his scent, that slight hint of cologne, it's hard to keep thinking of Ava. "I didn't know you were coming," he murmurs, taking my hand. "Come into the office."

I follow him, giving Sharon, who has gone back toward her desk, a smile as we go. I wait for the door to close behind us before I face Landon. "I didn't know you were still seeing Ava."

"Seeing Ava?" He looks slightly amused, which, given the circumstances, is infuriating. "I saw Ava this afternoon because she arrived here and wanted to discuss an issue pertinent to the Gold Dust." He draws me into his arms. "I'm seeing you."

"Yes, but…" I sigh, wondering what I was going to say. I don't want her around you? I don't like her? She still wants you? They were all 'jealous girlfriend' things to say, and I didn't want to play the jealous girlfriend, not when… Not at this point in our relationship.

I search his face. If she asked to see him, then it wouldn't have made sense to turn her away, not when she wanted to talk about the hotel he bought from her family. And yet, I can't forget the things she told me in San Francisco, her certainty that Landon would always come back to her.

"I thought she lived in San Francisco," I mutter.

"She does."

"Then why do we keep running into her here?"

Landon lifts my chin, so I'm looking at him. "Forget Ava. She's a part of my past that doesn't matter at all."

I look into his face. He loves me. That was what mattered, more than anything Ava Sinclair had said to me.

"I was about to have lunch," he says, dropping a small kiss on the top of my lip before releasing my chin. "Will you join me?"

"Of course." I force Ava out of my mind and smile. "What are you having?"

That evening, I leave my office early and get to the apartment before Landon. I couldn't stay long after having lunch with him because I had to get back to work. He'd let me go with promises to 'make me moan' as soon as he got me alone again.

As I let myself in, I realize how much I'm looking

forward to the fulfillment of that promise. I'll never get enough of him, of his touch, of his love.

I order dinner before going upstairs to change. I've become so used to being here, in his apartment, that it has started to feel like home. It's almost disloyal, how much I don't miss my own apartment. No matter what my misgivings were about moving in with Landon, I can't deny even to myself, that there was everything to love about the idea, especially knowing without any doubt that every day, I would come home to him, or him to me.

I fall asleep on the living room sofa, my ereader in my hand. When I wake up, it's to Landon's lips on mine in a tender kiss that goes straight from my lips to my heart.

"Hey, sexy," I whisper, my nose filling with his scent.

"Hey, baby." He's squatting beside the couch, his eyes on my face. He's still wearing his suit, though he has loosened his tie, and the top buttons of his shirt are open.

The endearment gives me a strange urge to curl up in his arms. "I dozed off," I say softly, reaching up to touch his cheek.

He kisses me again, and his lips are soft and warm. "Have you had anything to eat?"

"No, but I ordered dinner." I glance at my watch. "It should be here soon."

Rising to his feet, he shrugs off his jacket then sits beside me on the sofa. His firm muscles stretch out the crisp white shirt he's wearing, and I wriggle onto his lap so I can run my hands over his arms and feel the hardness beneath. "You're so hot."

He laughs. "For you."

Take that! Ava Sinclair, I think triumphantly, lowering my head to cover his lips with mine. Our kiss is soft and sweet, and much too short. The arrival of the food interrupts us and I moan my annoyance before wriggling off Landon's lap to take the delivery.

Later, when we're in bed, naked and he's kissing a path down from my neck, over my breasts, and down to my navel, his lips linger on the sensitive skin of my lower belly and he raises his head to look at me, his gaze strangely troubled.

"Do you still have doubts?" he asks. "About me?"

I shake my head. "No," I whisper softly.

His eyes stay on my face. "If you hadn't come by the office, I would have told you as soon as I saw you tonight that I met with Ava. You have no reason to be suspicious."

I sigh. I wasn't suspicious of him, but Ava was

another story. How could I explain to him that regardless of my best intentions, every woman, especially one like Ava, who had so obviously expressed her interest in him, became a reason to worry. Wasn't that normal, when one was in love?

"I'm no longer thinking about Ava," I reassure him, unwilling to let her ruin the rest of our night.

He seems to accept that, lowering his head and resuming the slow trail of his lips down to the juncture of my thighs. Once his tongue touches me there, I stop thinking at all. He uses it with a wicked expertise that borders on diabolical. Soon, I'm mindless, sweaty, moaning, and calling out his name.

After he makes me come with his fingers and tongue, he rears up over me, kneeling between my thighs as he lifts one of my legs over his shoulder. I'm wet and slick from my orgasm, and he enters me easily, stretching me with a sweetness that brings tears to my eyes.

"Landon," I moan his name, almost breathless with pleasure.

He doesn't move. "I love you, Rachel," he says, his voice husky. "Only you, tell me you know that."

I nod. "I do."

He drops my leg and lowers his body to rest on his elbows so his face is hovering over mine. "You have to learn to trust me."

I bite back a moan. "I trust you," I whisper.

He moves, once, pulling out of me and thrusting back in with a sweet, sure stroke, so deep, I let out a weak groan.

"Only you." His voice is a husky murmur. He rises back up to his knees, pulls my hips toward him, and really starts to move, stroking his hard length in and out of me with ferocious intensity. Everything about him is arousing, the raw hunger on his face, the sheen of sweat on his skin, the hard bunching of his chest muscles, the flat tightness of his stomach as he moves his hips, flexing, thrusting so deep inside me, that I feel as if I'm melded to him.

"Landon," I moan, about to unravel. "Landon." My voice is tight with desperation.

In response, he picks up his pace, his increased thrusts sending me over the edge. I cry out as my body tightens, spasming with the force of my orgasm, and he's right there with me. He thrusts deep, shuddering as he spills himself inside me, my name a soft whisper on his beautiful lips.

Later, when I'm wrapped in his arms, recovering from the haze of pleasure, I hear his soft whisper in my ear. "I never want to be without you. I've felt what that's like, and I never want to return to that dark lonely winter. It's okay if you don't want to move in, as long as it's not because you think I'd hurt or disappoint you. I won't. I'd die before I hurt you, Rachel, trust me."

"I do… I'm just… I'm afraid," I admit softly. "I'm scared of changing anything about us. Everything feels so perfect. I'm just so afraid of doing something to ruin it."

"I won't let anything ruin this," he promises. "Do you believe me?"

I breathe in the scent of his skin, the slight hint of sweat. "I do."

I feel his chest rise, and his arm comes around me to pull me closer, holding me like that until I drift off to sleep.

It's the thrashing that wakes me up, and the sound of my name, like a garbled plea on Landon's lips.

"Please," he's saying, his voice muffled yet somehow desperate. "Please. Oh God! Rachel."

I put on the bedside lamp, my heart breaking to see the tears on his cheeks. "Please," he moans, his body tight with the struggle in his nightmare. "Please."

I hold on to one of his thrashing arms, trying to keep him still. "Landon."

He wakes up immediately, rising from the pillows, his eyes fixing on the arm I'm holding in my two hands. I release it and he raises it to dig the fingers into his hair in a sad gesture of frustration.

"I'm sorry," he says. "I didn't… I was planning to get up.

I sigh. "You're not supposed to get up at night, Landon. I hate it that you can't sleep through the night."

He is quiet.

"Are they getting worse?" It's a hard question for me to ask. I'd hoped that being with me would make his past easier to bear, that I would make him better, not worse."

"It doesn't matter," he mutters. "They're just dreams."

"You were saying my name." I frown, unwilling to let him dismiss it. Not again. "Was it like that night in San Francisco? Was it me again, in the accident?"

"It was just a dream," he says, getting up from the bed and reaching for his robe.

"No." I protest. "Don't you think it matters if you're still dreaming of trying to save me and being unable to? If you're still afraid of hurting me? How can I…"

"How can you trust me, when even in my subconscious I'm struggling with the certainty that I'm somehow going to cause you pain?" Landon shakes his head in a silent gesture of denial and frustration then shrugs the robe on over his naked body. "Look, Rachel, I think we'd both be better off if you didn't try to analyze me. My dreams have nothing to do with you. I've dealt with them almost all my life."

"And you're still dealing with them," I point out. "And I'm dealing with them too."

His eyes close, but he stays silent.

"Fine," I say, raising my hands. "I'm not qualified to analyze you, but I think you should see someone else. I know you've had therapy, but remember what you told me in Newport, about how you thought, how you felt it was your fault… You said you'd never told anyone about that. Maybe…"

"Nothing…" Landon interrupts. "Maybe nothing." His voice is suddenly hard and impatient. "This is me," he mutters. "There is no guarantee that anything will ever be different. I try to be in control, but sometimes, especially when I'm with you, I get comfortable, and I forget to manage the memories I've carried around for more than half my life. But this is me, Rachel. My memories will probably haunt my dreams forever, and if that's the reason why…" he stops.

"Why I haven't said I'll move in with you?" I shake my head. "You know it's not."

"Why don't you go back to sleep," he says gently. "I'm going to try to get some work done."

I watch him leave. Not sure what to think. On one hand, I understand that he'd had to build his own defenses against the horror of watching his mother die, and that unraveling those defenses now would go against the steely control he has grown used to. But I can't continue to watch him come apart every night and not feel that we should at least look for a solution.

I sigh and lie back on the pillow, not bothering to try to go back to sleep. I'm still awake when Landon returns and starts to prepare for work, and I join him, both of us quiet, not talking about what happened. We have breakfast together, still silent, and it lasts all through the short ride to my office. Outside the Gilt building, when I reach for the door handle to get out of the car, Landon reaches for my hand.

"I'll see you in the evening," he says, his eyes searching my face. We're supposed to leave for his mystery weekend destination later in the day, and now, seeing the uncertainty in his eyes, it's almost as if he's afraid that last night would make me do something like change my mind, or walk away again.

But there's nothing that could ever make me leave him, not again, not ever. "Of course," I say with a small smile. "Have a great day."

"I don't know why you're drawing it out," Laurie is saying. "You know you're going to move in with him."

We're in the dressing room of a bridal boutique, whose owner is a former model like Aunt Jacie. My lunch hour is already gone, but I'm relieved that Laurie has already chosen her gown, a flowy, off-shoulder dream that's perfect for a beach wedding.

"I don't know anything, and neither do you," I frown again at the selection of bridesmaid dresses on the rack in front of me. Sissy Fletcher, the owner of the boutique, had selected them especially for me to view, or so she said. They were all beautiful, sweet pastel colors and girlish styles, the perfect accompaniment to Laurie's dress. I've tried them on, and they were all flattering.

'What are your misgivings exactly?" Laurie frowns. "Wanna share?"

I shrug, my hand hovering over one of the dresses,

then moving to another one. I don't know how to put all my worries into words. There were so many things that happened in a relationship - so many feelings, and tiny little actions that were impossible to explain to outsiders. "I just don't want to rush."

"So you keep saying." She looks at the dresses. "Want my opinion?"

"On the dresses, yes. On moving in with Landon, no."

She laughs. "Sometimes it doesn't take four years, you know."

I give her a warning look.

"What!" she exclaims. "You knew I was going to give you my opinion anyway." She picks a dress, then another, then puts them back on the rack. "They're all lovely. I can't tell you which one to take."

I sigh. "Of course." Looking over the rack again, I select one, a lilac off-shoulder dress with a sweetheart neckline and a hemline that dances around my knees. "We're still doing bare feet?"

"Of course." Laurie grins at my choice. "This was always my fav!" she exclaims. "See? I instinctively know what you want. Which is why I know you want to move in with Landon."

"I'm beginning to think he's co-opted you into

convincing me," I say, glowering at her. Inside, I'm thinking about Landon's face from this morning, our mutual silence, last night....

"Ha ha." Laurie rolls her eyes, oblivious to my thoughts. "I always have your best interests at heart." She thinks for a moment, then wrinkles her nose. "I've become one of those people in relationships who try to push everyone else into the same level of commitment, haven't I?"

"You have," I agree.

"Just think about it," she says, laughing. "Do what *you* want to do," She emphasizes the 'you.' "And no matter what, don't forget that you have a tribe, and we always have your back."

I won't, I say silently. I can always count on my family, and not just them. I think of Landon, and suddenly I know for sure that I'm going to say yes. Because I know, deep down, I can count on him too.

After work, Joe is waiting to take me to the airport. During our drives together, he has told me about his family. He has a teenage daughter, who lives with her mother in Connecticut, and he sees her about once a month. I ask him about her now, and he tells me he's going to see her over the weekend.

"Enjoy yourself," I tell him, catching the animation in his eyes through the rearview mirror. My own feelings are less straightforward. My mind keeps going back to last night, and I don't know whether to accept that as far as Landon is concerned, I can't help him with his nightmares and that I shouldn't bother.

I could live with them. I would gladly lie beside him and give him the little comfort I can for the rest of my life. What I can't do is watch him suffer alone, refuse to let me in, and refuse any other kind of help as well.

Inside the plane, Landon is in the bedroom, a tastefully decorated cabin with muted dark wood accents. He's having a conversation on the phone and I catch a few words while I stand at the door admiring him. He looks gorgeous - beautiful and golden. His sleeves are rolled up, exposing muscular forearms. His collar is open too, his shirt still tucked into his pants, but slightly pulled out and rough around the waistband. It pulls at my heart, how helpless I am about this attraction. I could look at him all day, and I'd consider my day well spent.

"Evans Sinclair is just a hair's breadth away from being committed. No sensible person is paying attention to him," Landon is saying, "and neither should you."

Even as he's speaking, he's walking toward me, and as his eyes hold mine with a silent question, I know that I'm not the only one still thinking about last night.

I raise myself on tiptoe to kiss him on the lips, and when I pull back, he holds on to my arm, his touch soft, but firm and possessive as he ends his conversation.

"You look beautiful," he whispers, his eyes flicking over my face.

I smile softly, deeply affected by the simple compliment. "You too."

"Beautiful?" he smiles and places his lips on mine, letting them linger lazily over my mouth. I close my eyes, enjoying the warm firmness of his touch as I relax against him. He sighs and touches his forehead to mine.

"Rachel…" he starts.

"Wait," I interrupt. I pull my face back and search his eyes, and I can see all my worry and uncertainty reflected in his. I know that whatever he has to say, it'll have something to do with last night, but I don't want that to color our weekend. "I'll move in with you," I tell him softly. "I want us to live together."

His arms go around me, pulling me even closer to his body. I feel his chest rise and swell, and I place my arms around his waist. "I was always going to say yes," I whisper.

"I'm glad… relieved." He leans back so he can look in my eyes. "I'm sorry about last night, for brushing off your concern. God knows I want to share everything with you. Every hope, every pain… but I don't want to burden you. I've become used to doing things on my own."

"You're not alone anymore," I reach behind me and take his hands, lacing my fingers with his. "You have me now, and I'm not just here for you to spoil and take care of. I want to share everything, the joys, and the pains. No matter what they are."

Landon sighs. "Lord knows what I did to deserve you."

"You didn't have to do anything. You just had to be you."

His lips cover mine, and he doesn't stop kissing me until a voice comes on over hidden speakers to let us know we'll be leaving soon.

The takeoff is smooth, and soon we're cruising. In the remarkably spacious bathroom, I quickly freshen up, and when I return, one of the stewardesses is wheeling in dinner on a tray.

"This weekend?" Landon suggests while we're

eating.

"What?" I'm puzzled until I realize that he's talking about the move. "Are you going to turn the plane around?"

"I can arrange for a few things to be brought over to my place, and we can deal with your lease next week."

"You're very eager to get me into your apartment," I tease. "I suspect you have plans for me."

His grin is telling. "Dark, dirty plans."

I wet my lips. "I can't wait."

His eyes rest on my lips for a moment, then he chuckles, and draws them away. "I can't even get through a meal without wanting to bury myself inside you."

I breathe. "I want you to bury yourself inside me."

His lips part, then he sighs softly. "My people can bring your clothes, books… over to my place, and leave the furniture for you to choose which you want to keep or give away… sell."

The thought of my apartment disappearing makes me a little sad, but the sadness is drowned by excitement, the knowledge that I'm moving to another level of commitment with the man I love.

"You won't regret this," Landon says. "Trust me."

"I do."

After we eat, he goes back to making his business calls while from the bed, I listen with half an ear as he discusses deals, alternating between demanding results and encouraging better performance. When he's done with the final call, I watch him run a hand through his hair and turn to me, his face showing his exhaustion.

"I need a new career plan. Something that involves lying on a beach somewhere, with you, naked, no phones..."

I snort. "You'd get bored… plus I have a new job. I'm not going to shelf it so I can lie naked with you on a beach all day," I pause as the image solidifies in my head. "Although it is tempting."

"Just tempting?" He gives me a teasing grin. "Now I know I have to up my game."

If he upped his game any further, I'd probably combust. "I heard part of your conversation earlier," I tell him. "Are you still having issues with Evans Sinclair and his libel?"

Landon sighs tiredly. "People love bad things to talk about, but hardly anybody takes him seriously. He seems to be getting more and more unhinged every day. He was running the Gold Dust into the ground. I saved that hotel, but he refuses to see that."

I remember the blind hatred on Evans' face during

our short meeting in San Francisco. The way he'd spit out the words that accused Landon of using his sister. He'd probably always resented Landon's relationship with Ava, and his loss of the Gold Dust had been the final nail in the coffin that consolidated the vicious hate. "Well, I'm glad he doesn't have the means to actually hurt your business."

"That's why I'm not worried. Although, I feel some sympathy for his family."

Ava in particular? The words hover on the tip of my tongue, but I recognize them for what they are, unnecessary and unwarranted jealousy, so I swallow them and hold out a hand to Landon. "You've got me for the whole weekend," I murmur suggestively. "What are you planning to do with me?"

"First of all," he grins and comes to stand at the edge of the bed, taking my proffered hand. "There's a club we should be thinking of joining."

"We?" My eyes widen with disbelief. "You've never done it here?"

Landon surprises me by shaking his head slowly, a small smile on his sculpted lips. "No."

The thought of being his first anything makes me excited as hell. I get up on my knees and place my hands on his chest. "So in here you're a virgin."

He shrugs. "I am whatever you want me to be."

"I want you to be naked." I give him a sultry look and start to unbutton his shirt. He helps me by shrugging it off, and my hands travel the expanse of his chest before I bend forward to lick his nipples, one, then the other.

I hear him sigh, his muscles tensing under my palms. Reaching for his waistband, I pull down his trousers and run my hands over the hard ridge in his briefs. He makes a soft sound in his throat, but his eyes stay on my face, watching as I pull down the undergarment and start to stroke him.

I feel him getting harder in my hand, stiffer, responding to my touch. Slowly, with my free hand, I start to unbutton my blouse, releasing his cock for long enough to shrug off the top and toss it on the floor, followed by my skirt, then my bra and panties. I hold Landon's gaze throughout, and when I'm naked, I reach for his cock again, stroking the full length once, before I cover him with my mouth.

"Fuck," he groans, his body jerking almost as if he's surprised by the sensation. He reaches for my shoulder, starting to push me back onto the bed.

"Hold on." I release him from my mouth and meet his eyes. "You're a virgin, remember? You have no idea what to do."

He curses softly, but there's also some amusement in his expression. "You're driving me crazy."

"I know," I whisper, pulling him down on the bed and rolling on top of him. I lower my body, trailing kisses down his chest and over his stomach until I reach his cock again. My tongue explores the smooth crest, tasting and licking, before sucking him deep into my mouth.

Landon lets out a long moan, his hips lifting off the bed. "I need to fuck you now," he bites out.

I replace my lips with my hand, stroking his full length. "You're very impatient for a virgin."

He manages a laugh, the sound turning into a groan as I cover him with my lips again. "Ah…" His voice is tortured, "Fuck, Rachel."

"Hmmm." My eyes meet the helpless, aroused expression in his, and before I know what's happening, he's pushing me off his cock, lifting me up over his body and turning me over so I'm face down on the bed. His movements are lightning fast, and in moments, he has my hands gripped behind me in one of his, and one of my legs raised to give him the access he needs.

I'm practically imprisoned, unable to move, as bound as if he's tied me up. When he pushes his cock inside me and starts to fuck me like that, I fall apart almost immediately, my whole body barely able to move, but shuddering with unbridled pleasure as his firm strokes push me to a screaming climax.

He keeps going, each thrust filling me with renewed pleasure. Soon I'm panting, calling out his name again and again, helpless as each firm stroke into my pulsing, needy heat drives all thought out of my brain.

"Landon," I cry out his name, desperate for release. "Oh yes, Landon!"

His movements increase in intensity, and he fucks me as if he needs to, as if he's desperate for something that's buried deep inside me, as if he'll never get enough of me. Pleasure peaks over and over until I'm too weak even to cry out. When I finally climax for the last time, my languid moan coincides with his fierce grunt as his body shudders and he reaches his own release.

He collapses onto the bed, his body stretched over my back. "Oh God!" he exclaims.

"Yeah," I breathe, my eyes fluttering closed. There were no other words.

The surprise destination is a five-star resort in Los Cabos. We spend the weekend lounging by the pool and enjoying the sunshine.

"Every time I go away with you, I discover another best place in the world," I tell Landon. He's rubbing sunscreen on my back while I sip a refreshing fruit drink that tastes like a burst of pure paradise. My body is sated from Landon's lovemaking. With his hands rubbing my back, and the knowledge that he's so totally mine, no work or other distractions, I'm practically in heaven. "I don't know why we ever have to leave."

"I can think of a few reasons," Landon says, "but you're right. They seem very inconsequential at the moment."

I turn around and let him oil my front, then he lays down on the lounge chair next to me. In swim trunks and sunshades, his strong chest and legs exposed, he looks utterly devastating, and it's clear that I'm not the only one who feels that way. I've seen the women ogling him all afternoon. Now, I can barely prevent a smirk from lifting my lips again. 'He's mine ladies, deal with it.'

I doze off in my chair, and when I wake up, Landon is also asleep. For a long moment, I lie there staring at his face, overwhelmed by the love I feel for him, and how happy I am.

He opens his eyes find me gawking at him.

"Hey," he breathes, smiling at me.

I smile back. "Go back to sleep and pretend you didn't see me eating you up with my eyes."

He doesn't say anything, but with one hand, he reaches out and pulls me over to his lounger. I lie beside him, curled up against his body. Closing my eyes, I breathe in the scent of his skin, and somehow, I don't believe that it will ever be possible to be happier than this.

10

The next week goes very fast, and the way Landon's people handle my move is almost magical in its efficiency. By the day of Aidan's opening, the move is complete and all the paperwork done.

Late in the afternoon, there's a farewell party for me at the office. It's a small party and Mark Willis manages to put aside his work long enough to give a speech about what a great assistant I was, and a hardworking writer and editor, while giving my replacement a meaningful side-eye. Chelsea tells me over and over again how it won't be the same without me, and the most senior in-house writers and editors just take their slices of cake and drinks and stay long enough to be seen before disappearing. Jessica Layner also shows up, joining the clapping at the end of Mark's speech.

After everyone has hugged me and wished me luck, I decide to walk back to the Swanson Court while Joe drives alongside me. Landon is not yet back from work, but the apartment feels like home even when he's not there, and I can see myself coming here every day for the rest of my life.

Landon has given me carte blanche to redecorate as I see fit, even offering me one of his assistants from Swanson Court International to schedule decorators and keep track of the work if I need the help. I'm not yet ready, but I'm sure I will be, soon.

In our bedroom, there's a large box on one of the chairs and a smaller one set on the floor, without opening them, I already know what's inside, and I'm not disappointed. Inside the many layers of soft tissue in the larger box is a beautiful dress almost as soft as the tissues. The small box contains a matching pair of shoes and a clutch. I'm still wondering who delivered them and when they came in when I see Landon standing at the door.

Giving him a quizzical glance, I straighten, watching him enter the room and close the distance between us. His jacket has already been discarded, leaving him wearing only his shirt and a vest. He looks delicious, and my mouth actually waters.

"You're back."

"Hmm-mm." He reaches me and lowers his lips to claim mine in a hungry kiss, one hand on my back holding me against his hard body. When he releases me, I'm breathless and flushed with pleasure.

His eyes rove over my face. "Do you like the dress?"

"Yes," I exclaim. "And the shoes and the purse…" I sigh. "You really shouldn't be buying me any more gifts."

"Try and stop me." He looks unrepentant and I watch as he goes over to sit on the bed, undoing his cufflinks and removing his watch before placing them on the nightstand. When he's done, he faces me, the corner of his lips lifting with an unmistakable gleam in his blue eyes. "Come here," he says.

I swallow, still reeling from his kiss. "You're trying to distract me."

"Come here," he says again.

"Shouldn't we be getting ready to go to the theater?"

"Don't worry, sweetheart. There's plenty of time." He shrugs off his vest and starts to undo the buttons of his shirt. "Come here."

I bite my lip, remaining where I am. "Come get me."

He moves as fast as lightning, rising to lift me off my feet before dumping me on the bed. I start to laugh, mirth bubbling out of me, along with a swelling of love that puts a little moisture in my eyes.

"You're so beautiful," Landon whispers.

My smile is soft. "That's love talking."

"Ha!" he scoffs. "You're beautiful by any standards, and totally my type. You," he traces a finger over my nose, "define my type." He lowers his head to kiss me, unbuttoning my blouse while he teases my tongue with his. I help him get the blouse off and raise my hips so he can pull down my pants.

"I've been thinking all day about tasting you," he tells me, hooking his fingers in the elastic of my panties.

I breathe, already helplessly aroused. I watch him drag my panties down the length of my thighs, leaving me exposed to him. My body clenches, eager for his touch.

Landon's face hovers between my legs, and I meet his eyes, sure that mine are full of excitement and expectation. His lips lift in just a fraction of a smile, a second before he lowers his head and I feel his tongue, a warm, velvety pressure on the most intimate parts of my body.

My head falls back on the bed and I close my eyes.

"Don't stop," I moan.

His voice is thick and husky. "Never."

Lifting my legs, he spreads them wider as he feasts on me, the relentless movements of his tongue a slow, gentle torture. I start to squirm and he tightens his hold on my legs and thighs, keeping me in place. I let out a helpless sound, my fingers finding the silk of his hair and clutching, pulling.

"Landon," I moan his name, helpless against the onslaught of pleasure.

He responds by flicking his tongue faster, moving one hand under my blouse to palm my breast, and the other to join his tongue, slipping a finger inside my wet center.

I make a sound, my whole body melting, surrendering to him. His fingers find their way under my bra, squeezing my nipple, while his tongue continues to tease me, making me go crazy.

"Landon," I beg desperately.

"Hmm." The sound vibrates through me and I pull at his hair.

"Please."

He raises his head. His hands leaving my body, but only for long enough for him to undo his pants. He looms me, positioning himself between my legs, the hard pressure of his cock at my entrance, pushing inside me.

"So wet," he murmurs, his voice a deep, husky growl. "So tight."

I respond with a moan, my arms going around him as he fills me, burying himself to the hilt, for a moment we just lie there, him, inside me, unmoving, with his weight resting on his elbows.

He kisses my neck. "I love you like this,' he whispers.

I sigh in pleasure, "Me too."

He covers my lips with his, so I can taste myself on him, and he starts to move, flexing his hips as he pulls out then thrusts back into me, each movement stroking my insides and causing a new wave of pleasure. He moves slowly, as if he's savoring every pleasurable slide of his skin against mine. My blood is on fire, my skin hot and dewy with sweat. My hands find his chest, my fingers stroking over the tense, hard muscles as he surges into me again and again. I meet his thrusts, my hips grinding wildly, wanting more of him, more of the pleasure. His eyes are closed, his lips parted as if in silent prayer. I hear him groan in one breath, and in the next, he whispers my name.

My hands flutter against his chest, pleasure making me nearly insane. "Landon," I manage once, my voice thin and feeble, then I explode, my climax bringing tears to my eyes. He lowers his body to cover mine as the waves rock me, then continues to move as they subside, thrusting with quicker strokes as his muscles tighten and his breath starts to come faster. I wrap my arms around him as he fucks me hard, nearing his peak. His orgasm comes with a throaty growl and a powerful surge inside me.

Later, after we've showered together and had dinner sent up from the hotel kitchen, we get dressed. Landon is ready before me, devastatingly sexy in a classic evening suit. My dress is black too, with a light gray embellishment that runs from one of the shoulders down to the flowing hem. Landon leans on the door to the dressing room watching me brush and clip my hair with the black onyx pin that came with the dress. I apply mascara and put on my lipstick, meeting his eyes in the mirror.

"What?"

He shakes his head, smiling softly. "I never thought I'd ever be jealous of a tube of lipstick."

I start to laugh, "You're unbelievable."

He raises his hands. "What's so strange about that, Romeo was jealous of a pair of gloves."

"Look how that ended," I say pointedly.

He leaves his position at the door to smooth my dress along the shoulders and zip it up, his fingers lightly caressing my back. "This, what we have, it's not going to be a tragedy."

I nod, leaning into his touch as I meet his eyes in the mirror. They are blazing with emotion, and the depth of my love for him grips me like a wave, making me feel as if I'm drowning.

"I love you," I tell him, feeling my eyes start to sting.

Landon grins. "Did my heart love till now?" He whispers in my ear. "For I ne'er saw true beauty till I saw you."

I roll my eyes. "You're bringing it on tonight, aren't you Romeo?"

"I can't seem to help myself."

I giggle and kiss his cheek. "We should be leaving."

His hands trail over my dress. "Fine," he says. "Let's go."

The drive to the theater is short, and Landon's hand is curved over mine the entire time.

"I forgot to ask…" he says. "How was your farewell party?"

"I shed a few tears," I tell him, suddenly a little nostalgic. "But, I consoled myself with the thought that I'm moving to bigger and better things."

"I love how happy you look at the prospect of editing short stories," Landon laughs. "It's charming."

"Oh shut up." I punch him playfully on the arm. "We can't all build hotels all over the world. This is my equivalent if you really want to know. It's what I've always wanted to do. Well…" I pause, "after I changed my mind from undercover agent and racecar driver."

"You're an excellent 'under covers' agent," he teases.

My mouth drops open and I give him a shocked glare. "I… I have no idea what to say to that!"

"What? It's a compliment!" He's laughing hard and I join him, happy to see him so relaxed. "When I was little, I wanted to be Superman."

"You and every other little boy."

"Well…" He grins. "After a while, I decided I wanted to be a pilot. I distinctly remember that. Not just any pilot, one of those World War II Navy pilots." He chuckles, and his smile turns a little sad. "Then I just wanted Aidan to start talking again."

His words make me quiet, and I lean toward him and plant a kiss on his lips. "You've been an awesome big brother."

"I know." He laughs softly. "These days I can't get him to shut up."

He can't hide his pride though. Outside the theater, he spends a long moment gazing at the sign with Aidan's name at the entrance, his delight written plainly on his face. I think again how lucky Aidan is to have him, how great he has been as a big brother…

He'll be a great father.

The thought sneaks in uninvited, and I turn my eyes away from Landon, unwilling to entertain it. Love leads to many places, but it's foolish to assume that it'll always lead to that. Especially when we hadn't even discussed *that* at all.

The red carpet event is dazzling, and I try not to gawk at Hollywood stars. After Landon has been approached by almost every prominent personality in the city, Betsy and Wilson Hayes join us. Betsy immediately envelopes me in a soft hug. "It's so nice to see you again," she exclaims, looking me over. "You're positively blooming."

I blush, thinking how Landon had everything to do with that. Wilson takes my hand, saying something that echoes his wife, then we all go into the theater where an usher directs us to our seats.

There have been a few changes to the play since the

last time I saw it, and the finished version is even more perfect. Elizabeth Mckay, the star, is electrifying, commanding the stage with a skill that seems at odds with her years. I sit beside Landon, so entranced that the intermission is like a punishment. When the curtain rises at the end of the last scene to show all the members of the cast taking their final bow, the applause is deafening.

"Your brother has a bright future ahead of him," a notable critic tells Landon when we go out to the lobby again. "I saw the whole thing a few days ago, and I couldn't resist coming back for a second look."

"I read your review this morning," Landon is just the right amount of friendly and gracious. "Even if it hadn't been my brother's play, that review would have intrigued me enough to add it to my schedule."

The man laughs. "Well, have a good evening."

The cast is still backstage, but as many people congratulate Landon as they do the producer, who looks like he's about to burst from happiness. I remember that Elizabeth McKay is his daughter, and I get it. The best part, I decide, is that after tonight, nobody will ever say again that she got the part because of her father.

Betsy and Wilson leave immediately after the play

because they're having a late dinner with some old friends. Landon wants to go backstage to see Aidan, but a couple of business types waylay him, giving me a chance to wander off to the mezzanine floor to find the bathrooms.

When I emerge a few minutes later, I find Ava Sinclair leaning on the balustrade outside. She's waiting, and from the gleam in her eyes when she sees me, I guess she's waiting for me.

"Hello, Rachel." She smiles. "How nice to run into you."

"I didn't know you were here," I reply, unable to inject any sort of pleasure into my voice. Why is she even in New York? As usual, she looks stunning, a blue evening dress flattering all her curves.

"You didn't, did you?" She lets her eyes drift over my clothes then languidly pushes away from the balustrade, falling into step beside me as I make for the stairs.

"So you're still with Landon?"

I let my eyes drift down to where Landon is standing in the lobby. From up here, he looks golden, beautiful, like a Greek god. I glance at Ava. "Obviously."

Her hand touches my arm, her face taken over by a faux look of concern. "But I warned you, darling, he's going to walk away from you."

"Like he did from you?" I mirror her smile of concern. "Don't worry, *darling*. I can take care of myself." I pause. "Since you care so much about Landon and me, why don't you ask your brother to back off? He's going around saying nasty things about Landon to anyone who'll listen."

Her lips thin, and her expression of concern disappears, replaced by thinly veiled dislike. "Evans is just jealous of Landon, of what I share with him, which you should be too, by the way. We've shared more than you will ever know."

Fuck you. The contemptuous words hover on the tip of my tongue, but I decide to be mature. "Enjoy your evening Ava, I have plans to enjoy mine, with Landon." I give her a sweet smile and walk away. By the time I reach Landon and enter the circle of the arm he leaves hanging casually at my waist, she's walking toward us. She's smiling charmingly in Landon's direction, even though some guy is holding on to her arm. His face is handsome and spoiled, his voice cultured but entitled.

To my relief, Landon is as charming and gracious with her as he has been to everyone else all night, nothing more. Thankfully, they don't linger, and I do my best to forget about Ava as Landon and I make our way backstage. I'm not going to allow myself to worry about her when it's obvious that she's clutching at straws to try to make me insecure about my relationship with Landon.

Backstage, it's like an arboretum with all the flowers. The commotion is out of this world as assistants and crew run up and down. Landon seems to know the way, pointing to the fact that he's been here to see his brother a few times. We pass the door that says 'Elizabeth' in block lettering, and there's a woman in front who looks like an assistant, telling visitors to return in a few minutes and taking delivery of all the flowers.

Aidan's office is at the end of the hall, but it's locked. We wait outside, Landon pulling out his phone to call Aidan, but before he starts the call, the door to Elizabeth's room opens and Aidan walks out, almost stumbling over the flowers and the overstressed assistant. His jacket is open, his hair disheveled, but he looks happier than I've ever seen him.

Landon has his phone in midair and his mouth drops open. I hide my smile and wait until Aidan clears the crowd of flowers with jaunty and carefree steps, before going to hug him. "The play was marvelous," I tell him enthusiastically. "You must be so proud."

He hugs me back, giving me a grin that's so like his

brother's it's almost unnerving. "I'm not going to pretend that I'm not ecstatic, because I am." He looks at Landon, "Though, I'm disappointed my brother is no longer duty-bound to get me drunk and procure the services of a couple of 'hardworking women.' That was going to be my consolation if the play bombed."

Landon smirks, and his eyes run over Aidan's disheveled clothes, "I believe you've consoled yourself fairly well.

Aidan smooths his hair, silent. A worried frown slowly creeps into his face, and I wonder if he's apprehensive that his brother may not approve, or if he's worried about his future with Miss Mckay.

"I think it's great that you worked out your differences with Elizabeth," I tell him, "You'll be working with her for a while, obviously."

He sighs and turns back to look at the increasing masses of flowers. "Yes," he says distractedly. "It's great."

He unlocks the door to his office. "Dennis Mckay is hosting a party tonight to celebrate the opening. Do you guys want to come?"

Landon looks at me. "Since I no longer have to get you drunk, I'm only here to congratulate you. Go to your party and enjoy your success, you'll be the toast of the evening.

Aidan smiles and suddenly puts his arms around Landon. "Thank you," he says, and I know he's thanking him for a lot more than just tonight.

My eyes are a little wet when we leave. Joe meets us backstage with the gift box Landon brought for Aidan, and after handing it to him, we head back outside. On the way back home, inside the car, Landon is quiet, deep in thought.

"What are you thinking?" I ask, leaning towards him.

He looks at me. "Just Aidan." He sighs. "The direction his career is going to go now..."

I frown. "It's going to get bigger from what I see. I'm sure you're very proud."

"Oh I am," Landon replies, "I'm also worried. The pressure on him will be so much. He has to follow success with success."

"But you have faith in him?"

"Yes, but..." he sighs. "Aidan is very prone to depression. He's struggled with it since… almost his whole life."

Since the accident. I sigh. Of course. Landon wasn't the only one who came out of that experience with scars. That day had changed their lives, all three of them, Landon, Aidan, and their father. I remember my conversation with Aidan, the first day we met. He'd alluded to his own scars, and credited Landon for rescuing him every time he gave in to his troubles. "Success makes some people depressed Landon, but not all of them. I'm sure Aidan can handle it." I lean closer to him. "Tonight, you should be celebrating, not thinking about the past."

He strokes my cheek. "You're right."

I cock my head, giving him a thoughtful look. "How can I take your mind off it?"

The worried expression disappears, followed by that heated blue blaze I know so well. "You know how."

I chuckle, excitement pooling in my stomach. I lift my dress so I can straddle him, placing my knees on the seat on either side of his hips and my arms on his shoulders. The movement takes him by surprise, and his eyebrows go up. "Tell me what you want," I whisper.

He gives me a look, then smiles. "First, I want you to stay right where you are," he says.

"Done," I laugh. My thighs are hovering over his hips, and I can feel his erection, hard and unyielding, already pressing into me, I grind a little and he sighs.

"The drive's not long enough for what I want to do to you."

"I know," I reply, grinding again. "I'm just teasing

you."

Landon chuckles then his hands flatten over my ribs, slowly finding their way up to cup my breasts. I lean forward and cover his lips with mine, running my tongue over his lower lip before sliding it inside his mouth. He kisses me back, taking possession of the kiss, as well as my senses, and soon I'm moaning and grinding against him, wanting so much more.

I groan when his hand slides under the dress, finding the damp crotch of my panties, and palming me through the whispery-soft material. My back arches and my body presses into his touch, wanting more. His breath is warm and ragged against my face as he hooks a finger into the elastic and pushes the barrier aside. The next moment his fingers are slipping through my folds, teasing my clit in a slick massage, before finding their way inside me.

The limo comes to a stop just as I draw my teeth over his earlobe, rolling my hips and encouraging him to plunge his fingers deeper. I look outside and we're in the parking lot of the Swanson Court. I hear the driver's door open and realize that Joe will come around to open the door any moment, frustrated, I slide off Landon, smoothing my dress just in time.

The door opens, and Landon takes my hand as soon

as we're out of the car, which is just as well because my feet are unsteady. In the elevator, he doesn't touch me. Instead, he teases me with a smile, raising his fingers to his lips to lick the tips.

"Oh God!" I moan, the gesture causing my lower belly muscles to clench sweetly.

"What," he asks innocently.

"Stop driving me crazy."

He comes to stand right in front of me, his body pressed against mine so I can feel his erection, hard against my belly. "Never."

The doors slide open and I shriek when he lifts me into his arms. He doesn't drop me until we're upstairs in the bedroom. He lays me gently on the bed, before straightening to take off his jacket. I notice the bottle of champagne chilling in an ice bucket beside a covered dish.

"We're celebrating?" I ask.

"Yes," Landon picks up a remote to dim the lights and turn on music from the hidden speakers. The soft, rolling sounds of vintage jazz flow into the room.

"Aidan's success?"

"And you, and me?"

He comes back to the bedside and pops the champagne, pouring out two glasses. He joins me on the bed and touches his glass to mine. "To you and me, to us."

"Us," I repeat.

He lifts his glass to his lips, then I do the same, feeling the bubbly tickle my upper lip. The teasing that began in the car continues while we eat, and somehow, Landon undresses me and feeds me caviar at the same time. It's sexy, decadent, and arousing as hell.

By the time we're both full of food and champagne, we're also naked. He nudges me back on the bed, kissing me long and hard, until I want so much more, then he leans over me to retrieve something from the drawer in the nightstand.

I crane my head and see him place a black velvety box on the bed. "What's that?"

"Shhh." He opens the box, then comes back to kiss me again, taking both my hands and stretching them over my head. "Do you trust me?"

"Yes."

"Okay," he instructs. "Close your eyes."

I obey and feel the flutter of silk as he binds my wrists, each one to one of the bedposts, then I feel him get off the bed, and a second later, he's binding my legs.

Excitement unfurls in my stomach. "Can I open my eyes now?"

The bed dips as he joins me again, “Yes.”

My eyes flutter open. Landon is kneeling between my legs, his cock hard and ready. A sound escapes me, like a moan. I want him so much.

“How do you feel?” he asks.

“Ahhh,” I sigh. “Expectant?

He grins and reaches for something inside the box. I only see silky straps before his hand disappears between my legs. I wait as he fastens whatever it is, two straps on my waist, then the other two going between my legs then up from behind so he can tie them all together, as he tightens the straps I feel the sensual touch of… something on my clit. It’s soft and velvety smooth, and when Landon adjusts it and does something to make it start vibrating, I gasp.

“Oh my God!”

“Do you like it?” His eyes are on mine.

My response is another moan. I’m incapable of movement, totally at his mercy. The device continues to vibrate, and the sensations are unbelievable. My body starts to writhe, caught between indescribable pleasure and the unrelenting need for more.

“Tell me you like it,” Landon whispers.

“I love it,” I manage.

He smiles, and leans down to kiss me on the lips, his

weight on his elbows as his lips trail down, hovering over each nipple before laving them with his tongue, all the while the vibrations on my clit are driving me slowly, sensually insane.

He lets one hand trail down my body, between my legs and over the little device pulsing at my clit, then lower. One finger slip inside me, and I groan as my body clenches around it, drawing it deeper. My legs start to shake.

"Landon." I'm begging, though I'm not sure what I'm asking for.

He looks up at me and I meet his eyes, my whole body weak with pleasure and need. "You're perfect," he says huskily, dropping a kiss on the heated skin of my stomach. A moment later, his finger slips out of me and I moan in protest.

"Shhh," he whispers, his hand moving yet lower until he's sliding it between my butt cheeks.

I resist the urge to ask what he's doing, concentrating only on the intense sensations I'm already feeling. When he slips something soft and lubricated into my tight rear opening, I cry out in pleasure. This too is vibrating, sending me into spirals of sensation that I'm sure will drive me mad.

"Oh God!" I cry out, almost frantic with pleasure.

"Landon!"

"Hmm," he replies, attentive to my every response. "How does it feel?"

"So good," I moan. My voice is thin and weak, and my eyes are trying to stay open. My whole body is shaking. I feel like I'm going to come any moment. "I'm going to come," I moan weakly, my body moving restlessly. "I'm coming."

Landon slips his finger back inside me, and I scream his name in helpless pleasure, falling apart as waves and waves of sweet sensation flow through my body.

His lips cover mine, kissing over my cries. My climax leaves me weak, and yet the vibrations continue. I'm drowning in a sea of pleasure, and yet I want more. I watch Landon rise on his knees between my legs and the sight of his cock; turgid and thickly veined, horizontal because of how hard he is…is almost enough to make me come again.

"I want you inside me," I beg desperately, "Please fuck me."

He positions his cock between my legs, leaning both hands on the bed as he pushes into me. With the intense combination of sensations, I almost come at once. I pull helplessly at the binds as he starts to grind into me, each movement of his hips threatening an explosion in my body. The way he moves, the way he fucks, it's as if he was created for this, to give my body maximum pleasure.

I hear my wild cries fill the room, my voice begging for more, screaming his name almost incoherently. I hear his grunts, rough feral sounds of pleasure as he nears his own peak, and then I lose myself, I lose control of my body, my whole being seizing with pleasure so intense that I almost pass out.

Or maybe I pass out. The next thing I remember is Landon untying me, and cradling me in his arms, the warmth of his climax still hot inside me, and the vibration of both devices gone. He lavishes kisses on my face and hair and holds me like that until I fall asleep.

11

The next day, I go through my work in a haze of pleasure, my face flushing furiously whenever I think back to last night and the truly indescribable sex with Landon.

I work for half the day and spend the afternoon moving my things to my new office. Liz Buckley checks in on me and asks me how I like the place.

"It's great," I tell her. It's nicer than my former office at least. It's bigger and the view is much better.

"I hope you still think so in a few weeks," she laughs. "Our deadlines may be harsher here than what you're used to. We publish every week."

I return her smile. "I'm looking forward to it."

Her eyes go to the flowers on my desk, lilies, my office-warming present from Landon. I'd told him my schedule for the day, so they'd arrived in the new office just after lunch. "Those are lovely."

"Yes." I look in the direction of the flowers, and sigh, not only because of how beautiful they are, but also because of how much I love the person who sent them.

Liz is smiling at me, no doubt interpreting the expression on my face to mean that I'm a lovesick puppy. "We'll meet later to go through your lineup for next week before you take your week off."

I was still very relieved that my request for time off for Laurie's wedding so soon after my employment had been approved. All I had to do was conduct an interview and write an article about the rising star of the Barbadian literary scene during that one week, which wasn't such a bad deal. I was already reading one of his books and it was excellent.

I start to say something back to Liz, but she's looking at something outside the office. "Ms. Weyland is here," she says in a hushed voice.

"Oh," I don't have time to add anything else before Liz is saying in a formal tone. "Good afternoon, Ms. Weyland."

"Hello, Liz." Gertrude Weyland's familiar face appears at the door. She's wearing a severe black dress, her black hair is up in a loose knot, her lips red and her face otherwise free of makeup, making her look years younger than her age. "How are you, Rachel?"

I haven't seen her since that night with Jack at her apartment, and now my mind goes to what Landon said about finding out if she had anything to do with me getting this job. "I'm great," I tell her. "Just settling in."

"Good." She gives me a small smile and starts to turn away.

"Ms. Weyland," I say haltingly, making her stop. "May I have a moment?"

She looks at Liz, who gives me an encouraging smile before leaving. "Is everything all right?"

"Yes," I say. "Yes, everything's fine. I just… I applied for a job here more than two years ago. I was a little surprised to get the invitation for an interview." I leave it as an open-ended question, watching her face.

"You surmised that I had something to do with it, and now you want to know why."

"I suppose," I say, feeling a little out of my depth. Her head is angled up, her eyes intent on mine. I try to read her expression, but it's impossible to know what's going through her mind.

"Let's say I did," she smiles a little. "What do you think were my reasons?"

I wonder how much she's enjoying this. "I have no idea."

"Do you always worry so much when you get the things you want?"

I stare at her, silent. I have no idea how to reply. Do I?

When I don't say anything, she chuckles. "You signed an employment contract that protects you as much as it protects the Gilt Review. You obviously have nothing to worry about. So why are you bothered?"

"I'm not," I deny. "I just wanted to know for sure."

She smiles. "I will concede that after our conversation the other night, I was impressed. Add that to the fact that you actually want to work here..." She shrugs.

So she had something to do with it. "Well… Thank you for the opportunity."

She makes a bored face and starts to leave, then stops herself. "You know that Jack is leaving Gilt?"

"I heard," I say noncommittally. I don't know how much she knows about my prior relationship with her son, and I don't want to make it a subject.

"There goes my grand plan of moving across an

ocean to be closer to him." She sighs. "Like all grand plans." For an instant, her face softens, and I'm actually sad for her and Jack, and the lack of communication that makes it so hard for them to have a real relationship.

"Well. Enjoy your week in Barbados, and make sure you come back with an excellent article," She arches a brow, and I find myself thinking of Jessica Layner, and how alike they are. "Okay?"

"Yes," I smile back. "Of course."

After Gertrude leaves me alone, I spend a few moments deep in thought, feeling some sympathy for her, and also for Jack. But ultimately, it's none of my business, and now that I've got my anxiety about her motives out of my mind, I can concentrate on my job.

I spend the next few hours arranging my desk and personalizing the office. There's a frame on my desk with a picture of me with my family, and another one of Landon and me. Laurie sent me a Doctor Seuss clock for the wall, which is cute and funny at the same time.

In the evening, I leave work early to get ready to go out to dinner with Landon and the Hayes. They are staying at the Swanson Court, but because of their full social schedule for the few days they're in town, we decide to meet at the restaurant instead of driving over together.

Landon arrives when I'm almost ready, dropping a kiss on my cheek before changing quickly into an evening suit.

"Look at you all sexy," I tell him when he comes to help me zip up my dress. He looks superb and he smells heavenly. "I don't know how you expect a girl to function when you look like a fantasy all the time."

"You function well enough for me," he says with a suggestive smile, making me blush. "I love the fact that you blush. Underneath all your bravado you're really a prude."

"We both know you couldn't be further from the truth."

"You know how you can show me how wrong I am." His hand curves around the swell of my ass and he leans in to whisper in my ear. "In fact I think you should remind me now, how far from a prude you are."

I ignore the frisson of excitement that moves through me as well as the sweet ache that begins between my legs, and concentrate instead on adjusting Landon's tie. "You're unbelievable," I tell him, "and if we don't leave now, we'll be late."

Wilson and Betsy are waiting at the restaurant, and the attentive manager leads us to a table with a spectacular view of the park. After we greet each other and take our seats, we talk about the play and about Aidan, who they saw at lunch. Betsy is fretting about how he must be stressing himself, while Wilson assures her that he's sure Aidan is having the time of his life.

We've just finished dessert when I see Landon's gaze lock on a table at another corner of the restaurant. I follow his line of sight, looking past a few tables until I see one with two occupants, one of them a familiar face. Evans Sinclair.

My eyes meet his and I recoil from the naked hatred I see in their depths. Shuddering, I shift my gaze to the other occupant of the table. He's an older man, unfamiliar to me. I turn my gaze back to Landon, a worried frown on my face. I'm wondering what Evans is doing in New York, and if it has anything to do with Landon, and I'm annoyed that a scumbag like Evans Sinclair seems to be about to ruin our evening.

Landon sees the look on my face and gives me a reassuring smile. His hand covers mine on the table. "More wine?" he asks, refilling my glass when I nod my assent.

He turns to Wilson and starts to discuss the Newport hotel. Wilson is worried about the viability of the project, but Landon tells him he's already drawn a contract up with the owners and he thinks it will turn out to be a sound investment.

I allow myself to breathe. If Landon's not worried then maybe I have no reason to be. I turn my attention back to our conversation, intent on enjoying myself, but just before we leave, Evans Sinclair's companion gets up, leaving him at the table, and on his way to the exit, he sees Landon and comes over to our table.

"Landon Court," he says, proffering a hand to shake Landon and then Wilson. It's been ages."

There is a certain gravitas to the way he holds himself, and I attribute it to his age and obvious success. He turns in my direction, smiles, and nods at Betsy and me. "I'm Devlin Barkeley," he says, still smiling.

The name sounds familiar, but I'm not quite sure where I've heard it before. "Rachel Foster," I hear Landon say, "my girlfriend, and Betsy Hayes, Wilson's wife."

The man smiles at Betsy. "I'm charmed," he declares. "I tried to hire your husband away from the Courts a long time ago. He wouldn't give me the time of day."

"He was happy where he was," Betsy replies, her face showing how unimpressed she is by the man's suaveness.

He shrugs, the charming smile still on his face as he turns back to Landon. "I stopped to congratulate you on your accomplishment with the Gold Dust. I have every confidence in your continued success."

Landon gives him a measuring look. "Your choice of dinner companion doesn't give me much confidence in your words."

The man laughs and looks back to where Evans remains at their table, glowering in our direction. "Evans is my godson. I owe him a fair hearing, but I owe it to myself to make sound judgments." He smiles across our table again. "Have a good evening."

I watch him leave, and a few minutes later, Evans follows him. He's swaying slightly, and I guess he's drunk. As he passes our table, he raises both hands and flips Landon, who ignores him.

After he has gone, I turn to Landon. "Who was the other guy?"

Landon shrugs, a small frown on his brow. "He's the chairman of a conglomerate that acquires and manages hotel chains."

"Acquires? Like takeovers?"

"Yes," Wilson offers. "They take the soul out of hotels and kill them with so-called efficiency. Sinclair there was probably trying to get him to try to acquire Swanson Court International from under Landon's feet."

"If he can," Betsy says scornfully.

I admire their confidence, but I look at Landon, wondering what harm a powerful conglomerate could do if they really wanted to hurt him and his brand, but then the man had all but assured Landon that he was safe.

That was something at least.

Landon senses my worry and gives me a reassuring smile. "It doesn't matter," he tells me. "He doesn't matter. The Swanson Court International is a very strong institution. I've dedicated my life to ensuring that. Even if Evans got a few people to sympathize with him, they'd be on a fool's errand trying to hurt me."

The conviction in his tone is both reassuring and in a way, sexy. We finish our dinner, and after Landon replies the maître d's obsequious inquiries as to how we enjoyed our meal, he leads me outside, his hand a light and welcome weight on the small of my back. Wilson and Betsy's driver is already in front to pick them up, and they go into the car after we exchange hugs. We watch them drive off, waiting for Joe to bring the car around.

When Joe arrives, Landon opens the rear door for me, waiting for me to climb inside before he goes around to the other side. I look up when he appears at the glass and starts to open the door, and then I hear the loud rev of a car engine. At first, I'm confused, not sure what to make of the glare of headlamps on Landon's face and body, then my heart explodes in paralyzing fear as I realize that there's a car coming toward him at full speed.

I watch as if in slow motion as Landon reacts. He opens the door and swiftly climbs into the car, shutting the door a moment before a black car zooms past, almost scraping the side of the car, the tires screeching as it comes to a stop a few yards in front of us.

I reach for Landon, frantic, wanting to assure myself that he's all right, but he's already pushing the door open. Joe is out of the car, striding purposefully toward the driver who almost hit Landon.

The driver is Evans Sinclair. I watch as he exits the black car. He looks unsteady on his feet but has an asshole grin on his face. I push open my door and leave the car just in time to hear him say in a loud, slurry voice. "Come on! It was an accident. I lost control of my car for a moment."

Joe has him in a grip, and Landon walks up to them, the barely controlled rage in his every step making me nervous. What is he going to do?

I take a step forward and stop when I see him jab a finger in Evans Sinclair's face. I can't hear what he's saying to him, but after a few terse-sounding words, he turns around and comes back toward me.

"Are you alright?" he asks me.

I nod. "He tried to kill you."

"He's stupid," Landon mutters, "and drunk." He opens the front passenger door for me, and I climb in, watching as he goes around to the driver's side. He gets behind the wheel. "Joe will drive him home and make sure he doesn't hurt himself, or someone else."

'Shouldn't you call the police or something?" There are at least two valets and the doorman for the restaurant who witnessed what happened. I frown at Landon, wondering why he's being so easy on Evans. He could have hurt you."

He starts the car. "Let's go home," he says tiredly, sliding the car onto the road. I look from his face to my hands on my lap. They're still shaking from the fear of moments before. Why is he letting Evans off so easy? I don't want to latch on to the closest reason in my mind.

The fact that Evans is Ava's brother, that Landon doesn't want to cause Ava or her family any embarrassment, maybe because he still cares about her.

The thought is unsettling, a dent in the confidence I have in his feelings for me. I shake my head, pushing my fears to the back of my mind. He probably has his reasons. Negative publicity would likely be as bad for him as it would be for the Sinclairs.

I watch his fingers on the wheel as he drives, the frown on his face, the look of concentration on his features, and suddenly, the profound relief that he's safe overcomes me.

He's not hurt.

He's not hurt.

I want to cry. I want to tell him to stop the car just so I can hold him.

At the apartment, Landon is quiet, his hand clasping mine as we make our way up to the bedroom. I can tell that he has a lot on his mind. We prepare for bed, and I'm still anxious, mostly because I can't shake the thought that Evans might be a real danger to him.

Landon takes a call from Joe, maybe to tell him that he has taken Evans to wherever he's staying. I listen to the terse responses on his side of the conversation, and when he comes to bed, I press myself into his chest, reveling in the comfort and warmth of his arms as he wraps them around me. My fear making me hold him tighter, making me wish that I could somehow ensure his safety forever.

The next morning when I wake up, Landon is not in bed. I felt him leave sometime during the night, but he didn't return as he usually does close to morning. I get off the bed, washing my face and brushing my teeth before I go downstairs in search of him.

The door to the study is open, and I hear Landon's voice before I reach the doorway. He's talking softly; his voice gentle.

"I would have called last night, but I didn't want to wake you," I hear him say. "He's your brother and he's out of control. It's time to stop talking and actually do something about him."

I stop walking, realizing that he's talking to Ava. I wait, not sure whether to go on, suddenly wrestling with the feeling that I'm intruding, which is absurd, or at least would be absurd if I didn't have that lingering fear about his relationship with Ava Sinclair.

"Ava," I hear him say. Am I imagining the intimacy

in his voice when he says her name? I picture Ava on the other end, beautiful, confused, and concerned, telling him how she doesn't know what to do. "I don't know what to say," Landon continues. "Try rehab or a sanatorium. The next time he tries anything like what he did last night I won't be so easy on him."

I turn around, heading for the kitchen. I put on the coffee and sit at the island. I should go back to bed, I think tiredly. It's Saturday after all, and what's a Saturday without a sleep-in? However, I know that I won't sleep a wink, not after last night, not after listening to Landon talk to Ava. My mind is in too much turmoil.

I try to shrug Ava out of my mind, recalling all the assumptions I've made in the past. I shouldn't let my fears get in the way of trusting Landon, however insistent they may be.

It's almost an hour before Landon joins me, he finds me still sitting at the island, surrounded by the aroma of fresh coffee.

"Good morning," he says gently. He's already showered, dressed in light pants and a gray sweater. His eyes flick over my face, full of concern. "Are you okay?"

I smile and shrug. "I'm fine. Good morning."

He looks like he's going to say something, but he

doesn't. Instead, he goes to the phone and orders breakfast. Esmeralda arrives soon after, with waffles and sliced fruit, before moving on to start her housekeeping.

I'm not hungry. A lot has happened to make me lose my appetite, but I eat anyway, my eyes on Landon, waiting for him to tell me about his phone call, anything to make me feel less like Ava still has some sort of hold on him.

He doesn't mention her, or last night either. I abandon all attempts to eat. "So what's going to happen with Evans?" I ask, breaking the silence.

There is a small grimace, like he'd rather not talk about Evans or last night." "Don't worry about it," he murmurs.

I stare at him, exasperated. "Of course I'm worried. I was there yesterday. If you hadn't moved out of the way so quickly…" I stop talking, the possibilities still fresh and fearful in my mind.

He sighs. "He's unstable and struggling with substance abuse problems. He's blaming everyone but himself for everything that's wrong with his life, but forget about him. He won't be causing any trouble anymore."

"Is Ava going to get him into rehab?" I ask, my voice

low.

Landon looks at me, his eyebrows raised in surprise.

"I was looking for you in the morning," I tell him with a shrug. "I heard part of your conversation with her."

He is silent, so I continue.

"The thing is, no matter how easily you brush last night away… I was afraid, Landon. I still am."

"Rachel…"

"No, let me finish." I hold his gaze. "It's not just the physical danger to you. It's more than that. I don't like feeling that you let Evans off because of what his sister still means to you."

Landon sighs. "Rachel, I won't deny that I tried to be considerate of Ava. Not because of what she means to me, but because I would have done the same for anyone else, especially someone I've had both a business and a personal relationship with."

Not because of what she means to me. He didn't deny that she still meant something to him. A vehement 'she means nothing to me' would have sounded like music to my ears. I stay quiet and let him continue.

"Evans is obviously battling personal issues," he says. "And I'm familiar enough with those to have some compassion for him."

"You can't seriously compare what he's going through to what you went through?" I say incredulously. "You witnessed an accident and blamed yourself when you shouldn't have. Evans is a spoiled playboy who is acting out his dissatisfaction in a dangerous way."

Landon inhales sharply then looks away. "Well, he will go to rehab, or go to jail." His voice takes on a chilling hardness. "Those are the options I'm going to give him. Either way, he won't be bothering us again."

I remember the screech of the tires, the cold hand of fear that had clutched at my chest when, for that one moment, I'd been sure that Landon was going to be hurt. I look down at my hands and notice the slight shaking, as if I'm still right there, in the car, watching the glare of the headlamps on his face. I close my eyes. "Okay," I whisper. "If you're sure."

12

Landon spends most of the morning working in his study. I return to the bedroom to shower before going out to the balcony to catch up on my reading. It's a beautiful day, so it's easy, after a while, to forget my anxiety and enjoy my book and the soft breeze teasing my cheeks.

When Landon comes out to find me hours later, I'm so engrossed in my reading that when I finally look up and see him standing in the doorway, I'm sure he's been standing there for a while.

He's still wearing his gray sweater from this morning,

and there is such a tender look in his eyes that I feel my eyes start to sting.

I love you to the point of tears. The quote enters my mind from nowhere, and I can't even remember where I read it.

Yes, I love him to the point of tears, because of how my feelings sometimes overwhelm me. I also love him to the point of joy, and laughter, and ecstasy.

And he loves me too, whatever Ava Sinclair tries to tell herself.

As if he can read my thoughts, he mouths the words. "I love you."

I breathe, my heart tightening as my lips lift in a tender smile. "I love you too."

He walks toward me, lowering his body onto one of the other chairs. "How's your book?"

I shrug. "Very good." I start to tell him about it. It's the book by Michael Davis, the author I'm going to interview in Barbados, and Landon listens attentively as I regale him with the details of the intricate plot.

"Are you really enjoying this?" I ask after a while.

"I love listening to you, especially when you're so animated." He smiles at me. "I ordered lunch. They'll bring it up here any minute, so please tell me more."

I'm so thrilled with the compliment that I almost

forget where I am in the story. I continue narrating to him until a hotel staff brings in our lunch and sets it out under Esmeralda's watchful eyes.

By the time they take the dishes away, my narration has caught up to where I am in the story.

"So what do you think?"

"I like it. You have to tell me the rest of it."

"Okay. Remind me when I finish." I make to pick up the book again, but he stops me, his hand reaching out to hold mine. "Not right now," he says. "Now I want to make love to you."

"Out here?"

He grins. "Why not?"

I forget about the book, allowing him to pull me up to my feet and down onto his lap. Soon I'm lost in the taste of his lips, the smooth heat of his skin, and the urgency of his touch. We undress each other then make love right there on his chair with me straddling him, and the mild afternoon sun teasing our sweat-slicked bodies. The balustrade is high enough that I don't have to worry about anyone seeing us, but I doubt that I would have cared.

Later, we get ready for a double date we have with Laurie and Brett. We're going to an art gallery opening, and then to dinner. My mom calls while we're getting ready.

"Sweetheart," she coos in my ear.

"Hi, Mom."

"How are you?"

"I'm great," I pause. "How are you?"

She sighs. "Working. Planning the wedding. Are you ready for next week?"

"Yeah," I nod, forgetting for a moment that she can't see me.

"How's Landon?"

I look over at where Landon is buttoning a light blue shirt. He looks gorgeous, the perfect epitome of sexy manhood. "He's great," I tell my mom.

"I'm thinking we should all have lunch on Sunday. It's been a while since you all came over."

"Oookay," I reply. "No problem."

"Will Landon be there?"

"I'll ask him," I catch Landon's eyes and mouth the words, "Sunday afternoon, my parents?"

He nods.

"He'll be there."

She sighs. "Good. Laurie, Brett, and Dylan will be there too, and maybe Brett's parents, they're not sure yet."

"How are you all getting along in the planning?"

"Very well," she chuckles. "Jacie is holding everything together so well. She's made two trips to

Barbados in the past month. If we were younger, I'd envy her, but, oh well."

We talk some more about the wedding, then my dad comes on to say hello, telling me that he can't wait to see me on Sunday.

After the call, Landon walks over to zip up my dress. I tremble when his hands graze my skin, marveling at how he can make me want him even with that small touch.

He turns me around after I'm all zipped, his eyes meet mine, and then silently he pulls me into his arms, holding me close like that for a few seconds. I wrap my arms around him too, content in our closeness. Somehow, I know he's thinking about last night, but I don't say anything, allowing him to take comfort from my touch.

"Do you know what I was thinking," he says. "That moment, when I saw the car coming toward me?"

I swallow and shake my head.

"I was thinking of you," he sighs. "Only you, and how I never ever want to leave your side."

Joe drops us off at the entrance to the new gallery, but after the opening, we all walk to the restaurant where we're having dinner. Our table is close to the window, and we make jokes and laugh while a few overzealous paps try to take Landon's picture from the other side of the street.

"Billionaire hotelier laughs while out on double date," Laurie suggests when we start to propose possible headlines.

"Or Landon Court bares teeth menacingly," Landon offers, "They'll prefer that."

"I don't know how you manage it," Brett says, shaking his head. "I'd probably retire to a deserted island and never show my face in public."

"I love New York too much," Landon says wryly.

Laurie nods. "Don't we all?"

"Your gym is growing," Landon tells Brett. "I'm certain we'll soon see things like 'Fitness king Brett Andrews spotted smiling on the sidewalk this morning.'"

"Ha ha," Laurie guffaws. "Brett will always be smiling though." She pats his hand on the table. "He's jolly like that."

"I am jolly." Brett agrees, nodding and pulling Laurie toward him so he can drop a kiss on her hair.

"What can I say?" Landon grimaces. "I volunteer as the scowler of the group."

I kiss his cheek. “I love your scowly face.”

We start to make plans for the next day, discussing and dropping the idea of going upstate together. Laurie has to go to the office to prepare some files for a deposition, so they might leave too late to make it by lunchtime, and since my mom will have a heart attack if we all miss lunch, we agree that Landon and I will leave without them.

The next day is cheerful and relaxing. My mom overcomes any misgivings she has about Landon to join Aunt Jacie in fussing over him. Brett’s parents make it too, and his mom corners me to ask me when the family will be planning another wedding. “I’m a romantic at heart,” she tells me. “I just think weddings, and I melt.”

“We’re not… We’re not there yet,” I stammer in reply, watching Landon in the dining room, setting the table with Uncle Taylor. I love him so much and yes, I want to spend the rest of my life with him, but even I know that we’re not ready for that yet.

Laurie and Brett finally arrive just in time for lunch, and afterward, Brett, Landon, and Dylan abandon us all to play video games in Dylan’s room. Laurie, who usually joins in, proclaims that the testosterone is too much for her and instead we all go into the study to watch my dad and uncle complete another game of chess.

Toward evening, my mom invites us all out to the patio. The season has already changed, and even as the leaves redden and the sun starts to set in colorful shades, there is still some warmth outside. We drink fruit punch and watch the vibrant sky, talking about Barbados. Those of us who've been there share memories, and Brett's parents express their excitement to go.

On the way back, Laurie and Brett stay in the back while Landon drives. We're all tired and a little drowsy, but Landon manages to stay alert, his fingers firm on the wheel. I prevent myself from drifting off by staring at him, at the perfection of his body and face.

"I love you," I whisper.

"I love you," he replies, with a quick, tender glance in my direction.

"And we love you," Laurie quips, making everyone laugh.

After we drop Laurie and Brett at their apartment, we drive over to the Swanson court. Upstairs in the apartment, we prepare for bed together, brushing our teeth side by side.

"Did you visit Laurie's Grandma often as a kid?" Landon asks.

I shrug. "About three times through my teenage years and once after college. We always went during the holidays, so there were festivals and stuff. It's usually awesome."

He nods. "What about your other grandparents?"

I smile fondly, remembering my grandparents on the Foster side. "My mom was an orphan when she met my dad, but I knew my dad's parents. They died a few weeks apart when I was about eleven. They had a farm, with cows and horses and pigs, and they built a treehouse for Laurie and me. We used to play ourselves into a stupor. Dylan had crushes on all the neighbor's kids. They were fierce. Hunter, Vivienne, Dinah and ah... Thomas" I giggle, remembering how Dylan used to follow them around. "He loved them all equally."

Landon is smiling at me. "What happened to the farm?"

"Dad and Uncle Taylor had to let it go," I tell him, a little nostalgic. "There was a mortgage, and at the time, Trent &Taylor was still growing."

He frowns. "Do you miss it?"

"I enjoy the memories," I pause, looking at him. "How about you? Did you know any of your grandparents?"

He nods. "My mother's mother was very affectionate. She lived in San Francisco and she would make up holidays so she could buy us gifts." He smiles fondly at the memory. "She died about a year before my mom. My dad's parents were retired and living in France by the time I was born. We used to visit them once a year. After the accident, my grandfather wanted to move back, but he was too old, too sick, and what was he going to do with two little boys anyway? They never really knew how bad it was with my dad, thankfully, they died about three years apart, when I was a teenager.

I try to imagine Lily Swanson and Alexander Court as an old couple. I'd read stories about them when I'd been scouring newspaper archives to learn more about Landon. They'd been a lovely couple, the media darlings of their time.

The image gives way to one of Landon and me, together, old, after a fulfilled life with each other.

The thought fills me with a hunger so intense my body almost seizes.

"What are you thinking?"

I smile at him. "Nothing really. Just what a devastating older guy you'd make."

He laughs and wiggles his eyebrows at me.

He looks so comical I start to giggle. "Come on," I tell him, taking his hand. "Let's go to bed."

Back at work, I have a busy week, with intense pitch meetings with the Gilt Review team, and racing to meet the deadline on my first article, a short commentary on misconceptions about women's fiction. I tidy all my tasks for the week as early as I can so that I can do last minute shopping with Laurie and my mom.

On Sunday morning, Joe drives Landon and me to the airport. There is another man riding shotgun, a silent, well-built man who is obviously an extra precaution for added security. He's been present since the middle of the week and even though Landon assured me that the extra security precaution was nothing to worry about, I still feel the ghost of Evans Sinclair and that horrible night outside the restaurant.

I slip my hand over Landon's and raise my eyes to his. In that first week I spent with him, I'd wondered how he managed to sleep so little and yet look as refreshed and alert as he always did. It was still a mystery to me. Years of training himself to need less sleep maybe? I sigh. He'd been sleeping less and less lately. The two nights I'd succeeded in convincing him not to get up, he'd slept beside me only to wake up a few hours later after having a nightmare.

Looking at him now, he couldn't be more different from the man I held in my arms until he went back to sleep. He looks so confident, so in control, that it's hard for me to reconcile the two images.

His eyes meet mine. "What are you worrying about now?"

I smile. "Am I so transparent?"

"No, but I've made it my business to memorize your every expression."

I flush, a smile curving my lips when his eyes linger on my face. His expression is tender and yet sensual. My mind goes to last night, and this morning, and the passionate goodbye we'd had in bed. "Stop saying lovely stuff to me. It's hard enough to leave you as it is."

"Then don't go," he says, with his own version of a pout. It should be comical, but it's damn sexy. I sigh. The thought of being without him for almost a full week makes me feel desperate too. He can't make it to Barbados until the day before the wedding.

"I want to turn the car around, take you somewhere, and hide you away," Landon continues. "I love Laurie and I know she's your family, but I'd rather steal you than lose you for a week."

"You're not losing me. I'm just going to be halfway across the globe," I laugh at his big frown. "Does it help that I feel the same way you do?"

"No. That just gives me more incentive to want to steal you away." He smiles at me. "I know I'm being selfish."

"You're not selfish," I tell him. "I'll miss you too, terribly. It's just… however tempting it is, we can't lock ourselves away forever."

His eyebrow quirks and a small smile finds its way to his lips. "Why not?"

"You know why not." We both laugh, and he raises a hand to trace his thumb across my lower lip. I see his chest rise as his eyes rove my face, as if he's trying to memorize every feature, and I can't help but feel elated, grateful even, for the emotions I see on his face. It mirrors what I feel. "I don't want to go a day without you," he murmurs, "ever. If it can be helped at all."

Ever. My heart swells. "I love you," I whisper. The car stops and we both look in the direction of the chartered plane where my family is already waiting. Then my eyes go to the front of the car, and where Joe and the other guy, I think his name is Collins, are seated quietly. I turn to Landon. "I need you to be safe."

"I'll be."

"Landon," I pause. "Will you at least think of talking to someone about your nightmares…?"

He is quiet, so I continue. "Whatever you're afraid of…"

"The only thing I'm afraid of is losing you."

I shake my head. "You won't."

He doesn't reply. His eyes go to my fingers still wrapped in his. "Why don't you start thinking of the kind of welcome you're going to give me when I do get to Barbados."

"I'll give you the tourist treatment. Show you the sights."

His eyes drop down to my body. "I know the sights I want to see, and I don't have to fly miles and miles to see them."

That makes me chuckle. "You have a one-track mind."

"You make me unable to think of anything else."

"I hate that I have to go now."

"I hate that I have to let you."

I swallow, and as if on cue, my phone starts to ring. It's my mother.

"I love you," I tell Landon again, pressing my lips to his, before reaching for the door handle.

He grips my arms as he kisses me back properly before letting me go. "I love you too. Call me when you land."

"Haven't you been getting enough sleep?" My mother asks after the plane takes off. .

I blink at her, blushing as my thoughts go back to last night, and the lovemaking that had lasted through the night and the early hours of the morning. I'd started dozing as soon as I got on the plane.

"It's been kinda stressful settling into a new job," I lie, not meeting her eyes. I'm grateful when she faces aunt Jacie and they go back to their wedding talk.

I finally wake up just before we land. Nana has arranged a car to take us to the hotel, a sprawling resort on the beach where the wedding will taking place. As soon as we unpack and freshen up, we head for her house, the hired car driving smoothly through the quaint cobblestone streets.

Nana's house is a sprawling bungalow in an ancient, but beautiful and quiet part of town. The compound is airy and full of fruit trees, but inside the house, it smells like wood polish and old books, and there are many books, ranging from fiction to history, which Nana used to teach at the University before she retired. There are also stacks and stacks of old copies of all the magazine issues in which Aunt Jacie ever appeared.

Nana wheels her mechanized wheelchair to the front porch but gets up to hug Laurie and me.

"Look how beautiful you two have grown," she says. She has a sweet, lilting accent, almost like poetry.

"Where is Dylan?"

"He has exams," I explain, "He'll be here with Brett on Friday."

"Ah, Brett." She grins at Laurie. "Congratulations again, my dear. He is a fine young man."

She turns her attention to the parents and we go inside to the large living room. Soon, Aunt Jacie's brother Ferdi arrives with his daughters, Berry and Tamia, who are a few years older than Laurie and me. They bring their children, who soon finish their lunch and start tearing around the house with that energy that children always seem to have.

They finally drag us outside to watch them climb trees. We leave the older generation in the living room and go to sit on the front porch, drinking cold glasses of fruit punch and keeping an eye on the children while we talk about the wedding, our bridesmaid dresses, men, and honeymoon plans.

"Where are you going?" Berry asks. She is the more vivacious of the two and she talks as fast as a runaway train.

"Venice," Laurie replies. "Dad and Uncle Trent's wedding gift."

"Lucky you," Berry says, and we start to talk about trips abroad and dream destinations. Tamia spent her honeymoon in Paris and Berry in Dubai, and we go on about the advantages of the beautiful cities. They soon turn to me to ask me where I would like to spend my honeymoon.

I laugh nervously. 'I'm not even engaged."

"But according to Laurie you have a guy who's crazy about you," Tamia's voice is whisper soft. "It probably won't be long now."

"Ha!" I exclaim, just as my phone rings. I can't hide my smile when I see that it's Landon. I get up to answer it, ignoring the meaningful looks from the girls. I'm glad to hear his voice, even though we've already spoken once since I landed.

"Hey."

"Hey." He sounds tired. "I just wanted to hear your voice."

"I miss you too."

"How's it going over there?"

"We're at Nana's house with Laurie's cousins, talking men and relationships."

"How very liberated of you all." There is a teasing note in his voice.

"What are you doing?" I ask, smiling.

"Working, and thinking of you." I sigh, and he continues. "What will you be doing all week?"

"Ah… Tomorrow we have shopping and I'm tagging along to meet the decorators. Then the next day, I'm going to be on my own, I'm meeting Michael Davis for his interview."

"You never told me the end of that story," Landon says. On his side, I hear a couple of quick taps, like typing on a keyboard.

"I'll tell you when you get here. What are you doing?"

"Nothing."

"Are you googling him?"

Landon laughs. "Of course."

I shake my head. "You're unbelievable."

"I know." He pauses. "He's very…"

"…Attractive?"

"I was going to say good-looking, but I guess you know better."

"You're jealous," I say, laughing.

"Of course I'm jealous," There is a smile in his voice. "Enjoy yourself," he says, after a short pause. "And let me know if you need anything, okay?"

I smile, "Okay."

After dinner at Nana's, we go back to our hotel. We're all tired, so we don't have any other plans apart from going straight to our suites. On the way in, the manager is in the lobby and he greets everyone politely before approaching me in particular, to let me know that he and the rest of the staff are available at any time if there's anything I want."

I smile and thank him graciously, even though I know that Landon probably has everything to do with the attentiveness. I tell him as much when he calls me just before I go to bed, and he doesn't even try to deny it.

"I do have considerable clout within the hospitality industry,' he tells me. "I'm allowed to use it to make sure you're treated like a queen." There's a pause. "Do you mind?"

"No." I'm lying in bed with the phone on my ear. "I miss you too much to care about what's going on around me."

"Ah," he breathes. "I miss you too."

I spend the next day shopping with my mom, Laurie, and aunt Jacie. We also make sure all the marriage paperwork is complete. We visit the caterers, the florists, and almost all the other vendors before Laurie and I finally beg off and take a walk through town, having an early dinner at a seafood restaurant before returning to the hotel.

The next day, everyone goes out without me. I sleep in, waking up much later than usual, but with enough time to make it for my interview. The hotel provides a complimentary car to take me to the university, where I'm meeting Michael Davis, who is even more attractive in person than he is in his pictures. The interview goes well, although I keep remembering my conversation with Landon and his admission of being jealous, and trying not to smile.

Afterward, I find the school bookstore and wander around, purchasing a few paperbacks before I return to the hotel. I'm surprised by how tired I am, and I'm almost about to nod off when Tamia calls me to talk about the all-in nuptial eve party she's planning for Laurie and Brett.

When everybody returns in the late afternoon, I'm asleep, but Laurie comes to wake me up, and we lie in bed talking about the future until it's time to join the rest of the family for dinner.

The next day, Brett and Dylan arrive, as well as Brett's parents, Brett's best man Jordan, who's also his partner at the gym, and Christi, a bubbly redhead from Laurie's office, who along with Tamia, Berry and me, make up Laurie's bridesmaids.

The dads spent the afternoon golfing, while my Mom, aunt Jacie and Brett's mom go over last minute details, like ensuring that everything Laurie needs for the wedding has been taken over to Aunt Jacie's old room at Nana's house, which has been remade into a bridal suite.

The party is in the evening, and somehow the suite I'm sharing with Laurie becomes the hub where we're all dressing up.

I'm ready before Laurie and Christi, so when they decide they need makeup wipes to repair a contouring error, I volunteer to go down to the hotel pharmacy. Once there, I quickly pick the wipes off the shelves, buying alcohol-free ones as well, just in case. I'm already on my way to the counter when something makes me stop.

I'm standing in the women's product section, and the shelves on my left are stocked with tampons.

Reminding me of the untouched ones still in my luggage.

I frown, wondering how long ago I should have needed them. At least a few days ago.

I breathe, telling myself not to panic, but instantly, my mind goes back to those two weeks when I'd been miserable, uncertain if Landon would ever come back to me. How many days of my pills had I missed?

Taking a deep breath, I look through the shelves until I find the pregnancy test kits. Back in the suite, I give Laurie the wipes, then go inside my room and use all four sticks I bought.

It only takes a few minutes, by the time Laurie and Christi are finally ready and we all go downstairs to the waiting car, my fear has been confirmed.

I'm pregnant.

13

I'm pregnant.

Throughout the journey to the club, I remain in a daze, unable to pay attention to anything happening around me, floating somewhere between absolute pleasure and tortuous uncertainty. The thought of Landon's child, my child, growing inside me fills me with a sense of delight that I can't deny, but we've never talked about children. Our greatest commitment is admitting that we love each other, and deciding to live together. A child is a huge leap forward that I don't know if we're ready to take.

I barely remember refusing the shots Berry brings to our table, or refusing the next round of drinks, and asking for water instead. Everybody else is screaming and laughing, having fun, but I'm spaced out, not quite sure of what I should do.

"Are you alright?" I look up to see Laurie's concerned face. "You don't look too good."

"I'm a little tired," I tell her apologetically, realizing that I have to pull myself together somehow and be present for her party. "I'm sorry. I need some air. I'll be right back."

I go back toward the entrance, stepping outside to the wide expanse of lawn separating the building, which looks like an old colonial home, from the quiet street.

"Are you alright madam?"

It's one of the bouncers. I wave a hand to let him know I'm fine. The last time I spoke with Landon was last night, and I know that today he's in San Francisco. As I pull out my phone from my clutch, I wonder if it's too late to call him, but I do anyway, because I desperately need to talk to him.

I wait for the connection, my anxiety mixed with the images of a cute baby with Landon's eyes that are starting to fill my head.

But… what if he doesn't want children?

What if he's not ready?

What if I'm not ready?

Apprehension builds in my stomach and I try to breathe, to calm myself. I need to tell him, to hear what he's going to say.

The phone starts to ring on his end, and he answers after a few rings. "I can't talk now," is the first thing he says. "I'll call you later."

"Landon…" I start to reply when I hear the voice on the other end.

"I suppose that's the girlfriend," she's saying. It's Ava. Her voice is unmistakable and mocking. "How like her to somehow interrupt…"

I don't hear the rest of what she says. I frown and look at my screen, and the call is still on. "Hello?" My voice is frantic as insane possibilities roar through my head.

"I'm here." Landon's voice is quiet. "I'll call you later."

"Who is that?" I say thinly, wanting more than anything for him to tell me that it's someone else. "Who's there with you?"

"Ava," he replies. There is resignation in his voice.

I don't say anything. Ava! Of all people, and of all the moments! I cut the connection, silence the phone, and place it back in my purse. My mind is purposely blank as I make my way back inside. Because I know that if I allow myself to think of Landon with Ava, of the sharp pang of jealousy making its way through my body, of the pictures rearing up in my head, I won't be able to be there for my cousin tonight.

I put in a good performance for the rest of the night, and Laurie and Brett have fun, which is what matters. After screeching at each other in the guise of singing karaoke, watching a troupe of male and female exotic dancers, while everybody gets pleasantly drunk, except me, we finally pile back into our cars and taxis.

Back in the hotel, Laurie sneaks off to Brett's suite and I'm left alone to dwell on Landon, Ava and the fact that I'm pregnant.

He loves me, I whisper to myself, trying to control the irrational feelings of jealousy, the pictures my imagination does not hesitate to conjure. He loves me.

I hear a vibrating sound. It's my phone, from inside my purse. I know it's Landon, but I don't trust myself to talk to him. My head, now that I'm alone, is filled with irrational suspicions. What if he's still with Ava so many hours later? What if the reason he was meeting her is something that will hurt me?

What if…

I breathe, pulling myself off that line of thought. I ignore the call and go to the bathroom to take a shower and wash away all the makeup and club debris. Maybe Landon will assume that I've gone to bed, and maybe I should. By tomorrow, I'll probably be able to speak to him without giving free rein to my jealousy and saying things I'll regret.

When I return to the room, the hotel phone is ringing, and I pick it up without thinking.

"Are you avoiding my calls?" Landon's voice is tight, almost angry. Immediately I get angry too. Why should I be the one trying to explain myself when he's the one who was meeting with his ex-girlfriend?

"How was Ava?" I ask pointedly.

He makes a sound. "So that's it, isn't it? You were ignoring my calls because I met with Ava? How about trying not to interpret every single situation to confirm your insecurities?

My insecurities? I bristle at the words. If I was insecure, I had good reason. "Why would I feel secure about the fact that you saw your former long-term girlfriend without letting me know? Even though you're aware that I have an issue with your continued relationship with her. Maybe you need her to convince her family to sell you a few more properties, or maybe she needs some comforting seeing as her asshole brother is going off the rails. And you're so considerate of her feelings aren't you, even when your safety is at stake."

"Don't be like this." His voice is serious, quiet.

I swallow and breathe, trying to calm my thoughts. "Why did you meet her?"

"Evans left the rehab facility, and I haven't been able to find out where he is. I thought she might know."

"When?"

"More than a week ago."

"More than…" I sigh, thinking of the extra security measures. He had known, but he hadn't bothered to tell me. "You didn't tell me. I was right there with you and you didn't tell me? You let me travel…" I breathe. "You keep treating me like I'm some piece of candy on your arm. I ask you to see someone about your nightmares, you don't. You have a problem and you ignore my input and the problem escalates but you choose not to share it with me." A frustrated sound escapes my lips. "I want to trust that I'm your partner, not just a replacement for Ava, the woman who somehow keeps popping up in your life, in our lives."

"Stop it," he says. His voice is somehow calm, even though mine has been rising steadily as I spoke. "You're making this much more than it is."

"Am I? Why did you have to 'meet' her? Why

couldn't she tell you on the phone if she knew where he was? Did she ask to set a date… tell you she'd rather talk in person? I'm sure she did, and of course, you couldn't say no because… Ava." I stop, angry with him, with Ava, with myself. Was it too much that I never wanted to hear her name again, that I wanted him to forget that he had ever been with her. Wasn't that love? Wanting to erase the thought of everyone that came before you, because what he felt for you made them… irrelevant?

"You're obviously not prepared to listen to me," Landon says slowly. "I have a lot to deal with over here. If you want to be supportive, instead of creating a scenario in your head and refusing to entertain anything else, understand that I have a lot on my mind."

"So I'm being unreasonable," I mutter. I'm suddenly on the verge of tears. "You know what? I don't feel like talking anymore. I want to go to bed."

"Rachel..."

I don't reply. I hear him sigh, a frustrated sound, just before I cut the connection.

The next day is spa day, and I push my conversation with Landon to the back of my mind and join Laurie, her cousins, and Christi at the hotel spa, where we are pampered to within an inch of our lives. That night, we go over to Nana's house to spend the night.

The next morning, Aunt Jacie and my mom come over with the stylist. The house is bustling with activity, but the room where Laurie and I are staying is like an oasis of calm. The stylist and the photographer work in silence, dressing Laurie and taking pictures. The other bridesmaids arrive and we get our makeup done and our hair adorned with colorful garlands.

Our ride back to the hotel is cheerful and boisterous in the two rented vintage Rolls Royces decorated with flowers, ribbons and 'about to wed' signs. At the beach, the decorators have managed to create a flowery oasis. Rose petals define the carpeted aisle, with bright plastic chairs on either side decorated with ribbons and bows. At the end of the aisle, Brett is standing with the minister and his best man under a white flowery arbor.

The parents and Nana are all seated in the front row, apart from Uncle Taylor, who's leading Laurie to the altar. One of Berry's little girls is in front of them, scattering more petals on the floor. I follow behind, walking slowly to the soft music from the band. Berry, Tamia, and Christi follow behind me, arm in arm with Dylan and Brett's other groomsmen.

I know Landon is there before I see him. The flutter in my spine is my first warning, then I get the familiar feeling of his eyes on me. I turn to my right and he's seated in one of the rows, dressed with the simplicity of the occasion in a long-sleeved white shirt and linen pants. He takes off his dark glasses as my eyes reach his face, and his eyes meet mine.

I almost stop walking when I see his tentative smile, but I recover myself quickly and keep on placing one foot in front of the other until I'm at the front. We take our seats while Uncle Taylor hands Laurie over to Brett and the ceremony begins.

I'm aware of Landon's presence all through, and it takes all my self-control not to go over to him, or at least retrieve my phone from my purse and talk to him, tell him how relieved I am that he came, how sorry I am for the things I said.

The ceremony is short and beautiful. Both Laurie and Brett cry when they say their vows, and I do too, though not as much as Aunt Jacie, who's practically bawling by the time they're pronounced husband and wife. Afterward, we take pictures, before everyone has to move toward the tables laid out in a large cabana.

Landon joins me then, while guests are congratulating Laurie, Brett, and their parents. He walks up to me and I sniff, blinking rapidly as it hits me all at once how much I've missed him. I'm going to have his child. Somehow, well I know exactly how, we created someone who would have something of both of us.

I should tell him, I know. I have no excuse for keeping it to myself especially now that he's here. And I will, I tell myself, once we're alone.

"Hey," he murmurs, when he's standing in front of me.

I smile. "Hey you too."

"You look lovely."

I sigh. "So do you."

An eyebrow goes up. "But I don't have flowers in my hair."

I reach for one of the flowers and stick it in his hair. It should make him look ridiculous, but it only makes him sexier. He grins, then his eyes lock on mine and turn serious. "I'm sorry…" he starts.

"No…" I interrupt him. "I'm sorry. I said a lot of things I didn't mean."

He takes my hand. "We shouldn't do this here," he says, looking toward the party. The children are laughing and chasing each other between the tables, and wine and food is being served. "It was a beautiful ceremony," he says. There is some wistfulness in his eyes.

"Yes, it was." We stand there looking at each other. "When did you arrive?" I ask finally.

"Last night. Much too late to do anything after the manager told me you weren't in your room. I had breakfast with the men in your family this morning."

"Oh!" That must have been after my mom came over to Nana's. She must not have known that Landon was around, or she would have told me. "I'm glad you came," I whisper softly.

He raises a hand to touch my cheek, gently stroking it. "I wouldn't dream of missing something so important to you."

The party progresses nicely after that. The best man gives a hilarious toast that makes Brett squirm in embarrassment throughout, and afterward there's dancing. I dance with my brother, my dad, Uncle Taylor, and a couple of other people that I don't know. Before Landon takes over and doesn't release me to anyone else.

The DJ switches to dancehall beats and Landon shows a surprising willingness to shake it to the dance tracks, as well as amazing skill. It's easy to forget everything and just have fun, to eat so much cake it's almost indecent, to laugh as Nana winks at me when I finally introduce Landon to her, and dance in a circle when Berry and Tamia's children insist on dancing with Landon and me.

Finally, Laurie and Brett leave. They're spending the night at another hotel, far away from family. From there they're flying to Venice. We remain at the beach for a while after they leave, waiting till the sun starts to set before we all say our goodbyes.

Landon follows me to the suite I shared with Laurie. He took a suite for himself when he arrived, but he shows no desire to leave me. I wonder if we're going to talk about our fight now. It was so great to see him enjoying himself that I don't want to spoil it by remembering anything else.

"I have sand everywhere," I tell him, once we're inside the room. I'm smiling, trying to keep things light.

"Yes, I probably need a shower too." He starts to take off his shirt. "My clothes are in my suite."

I raise my brows. "Do you think you'll need them?"

He grins. "Come on," he says, pulling me into the bathroom, where we shed the sandy clothes before getting in the shower. Landon kisses me under the warm spray and spends the next few minutes soaping my body so thoroughly that when I emerge, I'm not only clean, I'm also nearly incapacitated with arousal.

When we're both back in the room, wrapped in robes, Landon sits beside me on the bed. He has called the manager and arranged for his things to be sent down first thing in the morning, so he won't be doing a walk of shame in the bathrobe, an image that makes my lips quirk in amusement.

"About Thursday night…" he says, looking at me.

I breathe, my smile disappearing. I search his face, trying to be secure in the knowledge that he loves me, that he'll never do anything to hurt me.

"I love you," he says, his voice so soft and tender that immediately my eyes start to tear up. "I need you to know that. I need you to know that I'll never do anything consciously, deliberately to hurt you. There is nothing as important to me as you are."

I nod, tears in my eyes.

"I should have told you I was going to see Ava, and I should have told you why. I was hoping that I'd have been able to resolve the whole situation with Evans before coming here, and you'd never need to know that he was missing." He sighs. "Of course that was wrong as well."

"At least I know now…" I reach for his hand. "You still haven't found him?"

He shakes his head. "I have no idea what he's doing

or planning, and Ava refuses to get the police involved. With his drug use, he's irrational and unpredictable, and it's been such a relief that you were here while I was trying to find him, because at least I know you're safe."

"What about you?" I close my eyes. "There's a madman on the loose who blames you for his life choices, and I've been partying over here, with no knowledge of that. It makes me feel useless."

"I understand that now, and I'm sorry I didn't think of it that way before. I didn't want to ruin the experience of your cousin's wedding for you."

"I'm not a child you protect from everything, Landon."

"I know."

"So Ava didn't know where he was?"

"If she did, I couldn't get it out of her. She may not be crazy like her brother, but she likes to play games. I'm sure she knows where he is, or has an idea, and coaxing it out of her was the objective of meeting her for dinner."

"So you were trying to seduce it out of her."

"Not seduce." He gives me an appealing look. "Coax."

I breathe, deciding to trust him, even though the image of him with her, flattering her ego and trying to make her feel that she was important to him, enough for her to tell him what he wanted to know, it makes me clench my fingers. "But you didn't succeed."

"She admits that she gave him some money, and he told her he wanted to travel and 'get away from it all.'"

Travel. Hopefully out of our lives for good. "Do you believe her?"

"Maybe, but I don't believe him."

That night outside the restaurant comes back to my mind, and the thought of what could have happened. I remember Evans's voice in my ear all those months ago in San Francisco, how bitter he'd been, and filled with hate. I shudder.

"You understand why I had to meet her," Landon asks.

I nod. "I do."

"We have something special, Rachel. I want to know you won't ever let anything like suspicion make you think of throwing it away."

Again.

The image of two little boys wrapped in blankets comes unbidden to my head, and Landon outside my apartment, frantic as he waited for his driver to find me, for me to return. I know how much it means to him, to know that I will trust him first and not let my suspicions make me do something irrational.

"I'll never walk away from you," I tell him.

His chest rises, and in the next moment he pulls me onto his lap. "I've missed you," he tells me. "It took a lot of control for me not to steal you away from Laurie's wedding and find some corner to fuck you senseless."

"Jesus!" I laugh at the image. "Well. I'm glad you didn't." I wet my lips. "Although you can feel free to do so now."

He's already loosening the belt of my robe. "I intend to." He pulls the robe off my shoulders to expose my breasts.

My nipples harden under his tender gaze. "I love how responsive you are to me," he says. He parts my legs gently. "Your body was made for my touch."

"Yours was made to drive me crazy."

He grins and slides one hand between my legs. I'm already wet, and his finger slides easily between my folds. "God, I need to fuck you," he sighs.

"Feel free."

His lips cover mine hungrily, and at the same time, he starts to work me with his fingers. Two fingers slide inside me, while his thumb moves over my clit, rubbing and massaging with just enough pressure to make my body start to writhe. Sensations flood me, and I move my hips to the rhythm of his fingers, also feeling his cock hard against my buttocks. I moan. I need him inside me.

Landon reads my mind, because right then he rises to his feet, lifting me and placing me on the bed. He pulls off his robe with an urgency that's arousing by itself, and I spread my legs, opening myself up to him. He lowers his head between my legs, and I'm already so aroused that when his tongue flicks over my clit, I almost come, my hips bucking into his face.

"I want you now," I tell him urgently.

He kneels between my legs and fists his cock for a moment, before pulling me up by my thighs and sliding deep inside me with one firm thrust.

My already pulsing insides welcome him in, closing around him, urging him deeper. I close my eyes, surrendering my body to him, to the pleasure of his cock deep inside me. He starts to move in firm, hard strokes, and his hunger for me is evident in the way he fucks me, his hips jerking as he thrusts into me.

His fingers tighten on my thighs, and when my eyes flutter open, his own are narrowed to dazed slits, his breaths coming from parted lips. I tighten my legs around his waist, eager to see him lose control. "Fuck me hard," I whisper, pushing my hips to meet his thrusts. I feel my climax coming and I hug my breasts, my body tightens, and heat explodes in my core as I lose myself. He comes at the same time, his body jerking forward as an agonized moan rips from his lips, and he falls forward, dropping my legs, and covering one breast with his lips, even as the heat of his release fills me.

"God!" He breathes later, his arms tight around me. "I hope you never find out that you'd only have to say the word to make me your willing sex slave." He kisses my hair with a soft laugh.

I kiss his neck. "Now you've told me, I'll keep it in mind."

"I love you," he says fervently. "More than anything."

"You're everything," I whisper. "I can't bear the thought of being without you."

"You're never getting rid of me."

I sigh and relax into his arms. Somewhere inside, a small voice reminds me that I still haven't told him that I'm pregnant, but I ignore it. I'll tell him when I'm sure, I decide, luxuriating in the feel of him surrounding me as I fall into a peaceful sleep.

14

All the way back to New York, I wrestle with my irrational reluctance to tell Landon about the baby. Mentally, I can't even explain to myself why I'm hesitant. There's no reason I can't just come out and say it.

Landon, I'm pregnant.

How hard could it be? What was the worst that could happen? I sincerely doubt that he would conclude that he's not ready for the level of commitment that having a baby means. That scenario doesn't even gel with the Landon I know.

What if he decides to take responsibility but silently blames me for making him a father when he's not ready?

I sigh.

"Are you fretting about something again?" Landon is sitting beside me on the plane. He'd been reading on his tablet, but now he's looking at me, his beautiful cobalt eyes holding mine. Our child could have eyes like his, I think, the thought filling me with longing.

"No," I answer his question. "No, I'm just thinking about work."

Landon continues to look at me, his eyes questioning, and I turn away from his searching gaze, not because I think he can read my mind but because I feel almost as if I'm lying to him, deceiving him.

"No matter what you're thinking, about us," he says. "You can tell me and we'll talk about it."

I smile and take his hand. Squeezing it gently, and hoping he can feel how much I love him, even in that touch.

I doze off watching him read, and only wake up when we're back in New York. In the car, Landon continues to work on his tablet until we get to the entrance of the Swanson Court.

I know something is wrong long before we reach the awning. There is an enormous crowd in front of the hotel and it takes a moment for me to realize that they're reporters. They notice the car approaching and throng around it, their mouths moving from across the glass as they scream their questions, which I can't hear from inside the car.

Joe manages to get the car to the entrance, but Landon is silent, his mouth drawn into an impatient, irritated line.

"What's going on?" I ask, even as I realize that we won't know the answer to my question until we come out of the car, to face the mob.

"I don't know," Landon replies.

"Do you want me to go into the parking lot?" Joe asks quietly.

Landon frowns. "No. Whatever it is, it's better if we don't look as if we're running away from it."

Joe nods and stops the car in front of the doors. Immediately, the crowd swarms around it, and through the tinted glass, I can see the flashes as they take pictures.

"Wait here," Landon tells me, opening his door and stepping out of the car, with Joe following his lead. There's a sudden explosion of sound, which is cut short when the doors close. Then they both appear at my door, along with some of the security personnel from the hotel, who make a path between the sea of reporters, all of them flanking me as we move toward the entrance.

The questions are rapid, melting into each other. I hear Landon's name, over and over, and Ava Sinclair's.

Were you involved?

Did you have something to do with it?

Did you know?

Do you have anything to say?

Why is she asking for you?

Landon ignores them until we're inside the doors. In the lobby, Jed Fray, Landon's head of security, is waiting for us.

"What happened?" Landon's voice is an icy bark.

"We are working to get rid of them," Jed gestures toward the reporters outside the door. I haven't had much cause to talk to him before, but if I had to describe him, I'd pick unflappable as the most suitable word.

"That is not what I asked," Landon says tersely, obviously not impressed with Jed's handling of the situation.

Jed nods. He looks at me, then turns back to Landon. "Ava Sinclair was stabbed this morning in her suite at the Gold Dust in San Francisco.

Landon stiffens, his entire expression and posture

changing as Jed continues. "She's currently in intensive care, and we know the attacker was her brother. She was obviously expecting him. The tapes show that she let him into her suite…" he stops. "She started asking for you as soon as the paramedics got there. That, coupled with the fact that it happened in your hotel, and," He looks at me again. "Your prior relationship with the victim, the press are trying to make a story out of it."

I'm looking at Landon, watching that familiar pained expression take over his features. His eyes are on me, but it's almost as if he's looking through me. I swallow, willing myself not to wonder why Ava was staying at the Gold Dust, not to wonder if she'd been there when Landon was in San Francisco. The thought of them together… Spending the night under the same roof… It makes me feel desperate. I close my eyes, willing myself to be concerned for Ava's safety instead.

"How is she?" I ask Jed, surprised at how firm my voice sounds.

"She's in intensive care, but from the reports I'm getting, they're sure she'll be fine."

"And Evans?"

"They don't know where he is."

"You'll shut this down?" I ask Jed, pointing to the horde outside the door."

"Already on it."

I turn to Landon. "Come on," I tell him, "Let's go up, and decide what we're going to do."

He follows me to the elevators, silent. I don't need anyone to tell me that he's blaming himself for what happened to Ava.

In the apartment, I fix him a drink and he takes it from me, his face drawn. Esmeralda is already in our room unpacking our things and I realize that I probably need to ask her to pack for another trip. I still have one day before I have to go back to work. I'd thought I would spend it with Landon, but now that doesn't seem likely.

I watch him drink some of the scotch I gave him. "Please don't blame yourself," I urge, recognizing the note of pleading in my voice. "There's already so much you feel responsible for."

"But I am responsible." His voice is tight with emotion. "She was meeting him, probably trying to talk him out of his insane vendetta, and he stabbed her, his own sister, because I put her in a position where he saw her as an enemy."

"Landon, he's clearly insane. You can't blame yourself for that."

"Can't I?" he downs the Scotch. "He wasn't insane

before I bought the Gold Dust out from under him. He was happily running it into the ground, but at least he was sane."

"Landon…"

"Don't you see how messed up everybody around me is? Evans is crazy. Ava is fighting for her life. Aidan is dealing with severe depression… did you know that?" His eyes are dark with pain. "Sometimes he goes off the rails and disappears for days." He laughs bitterly. "You already know about my mother and my father… That miserable… We might as well have killed him, you know? Me and Aidan. That's why Aidan can't bear to look at himself at times. The last thing he told our father was that we were all better off without his alcoholic, useless presence, and I stood there and said nothing, because I felt the same. Maybe I thought there was some truth in the stories that drove my mother to her death. Maybe I was sick of watching him drink himself to death while ignoring his sons." He shakes his head, "But I stood there while Aidan shredded him, and the next morning he was dead."

"Stop this…" I whisper.

"How long before it's you?" His eyes are desperate, hopeless. "Aren't you afraid that you'll end up like us?"

"No." I take both his hands in mine. "Because I

don't see anything wrong with you, Landon. I love you."

He ignores me and rises to his feet. "I need another drink."

I get up and face him. Somewhere inside, something is tugging at me, some insecure thought. He's unraveling because of Ava, because he's devastated, because he still loves her, because… I silence the thought. "Stop feeling sorry for yourself," I say firmly. "This is not the time to fall apart. Think of the negative press, the questions people will ask about the security at the Gold Dust. Think of the fact that Evans is on the run, think of how much he hates you. You have to pull yourself together and manage this."

Landon sighs and lowers himself back on the seat. His eyes close and I swallow a lump of pain. He's falling apart because of her. My hand goes to my belly, hovering protectively over where my child is growing. Our child.

"I'm going to ask Jed to call the pilot and make sure you're ready to leave in a few hours," I whisper. "The whole world knows she was asking for you. You have to go."

Landon nods and opens his eyes, and I remove my hand from my belly, afraid that he may have caught the gesture, but once again, it's almost as if he's looking through me. I'm going to have a baby. The words play at my lips, but it doesn't feel right to tell him now, when he's so haunted by another woman's pain.

A woman he still cares about, obviously.

"You're right," he says. "Of course. I have to go."

I nod. My mind churning with all the insecurities I'm trying to push aside. Ava is the damsel in distress, and when my prince rides to the rescue, would he become her prince? Was a prince allowed to rescue more than one damsel? Who decided which damsel would get the happy-ever-after?

I almost laugh, the turmoil in my heart verging on hysterical. I have to call Jed. I have to arrange for the plane and tell Esmeralda to pack a suitcase for Landon. I start to walk away, but Landon's voice stops me.

"Will you come with me?"

I turn back to face him, and this time, he's really looking at me, and there is entreaty in his blue gaze.

I close my eyes. "Of course."

In San Francisco, a car is waiting at the airport to take us straight to the hospital. Outside, a respectable distance from the entrance, there's another small crowd of press and photographers.

I follow Landon inside, ignoring the camera flashes. An orderly leads us to the ward, outside which there's a small group of people I assume to be some of the Sinclairs. They greet Landon, but not very warmly, and they totally ignore me, which is fine, as far as I'm concerned.

A doctor soon arrives.

"You're Landon Court?"

"Yes," Landon replies, taking the doctor's proffered hand. She is looking at him with a mixture of respect and admiration, and I wonder vaguely if the hospital is one of those he sponsors. "How is she?"

"She's asleep right now as you can see," the doctor replies, pointing a hand toward the window of the private ward where Ava is. "And she's healing nicely. The attacker missed any major organs, so she'll be out of here in a couple of days."

I tune out the rest of the words. Through the open shutters, I can see Ava, looking small and weak in her bed, hooked up to a variety of machines.

Landon's eyes are turned in the same direction. There's no way he won't hold himself responsible, I think sadly.

The doctor says something else to Landon, which I don't catch, then she turns and walks away.

"She looks…" I shake my head, unable to reconcile the figure on the bed to the beautiful, confident woman I remember.

"I know." Landon's voice is grave and his eyes are shuttered. "You should go back to the hotel. I'll wait and talk to her when she wakes."

I swallow, trying hard not to submit to that feeling of being relegated, again. "Of course." I lean forward and place a soft kiss on his cheek. "I'll see you later."

The driver is waiting for me downstairs. At the Gold Dust, Claude Devin is solicitous but mostly quiet, so unlike his usual delightful self. As he personally escorts me to the penthouse suite, I feel a small surge of pity for him. It can't be good for a manager that such an attack occurred during his watch. I undress slowly, tiredly, before stepping into the shower. I remain there for a long time, letting the water wash over my body.

We have to trust each other.

I was trusting Landon, believing, and holding on to every reason he'd ever given to make me believe that he loved me. I'm holding on to all the reasons why I can't let myself think that maybe, just maybe, Ava was more important to him than I could bear; all the reasons why

I had promised him that I would never walk away again.

Not that I wanted to. How could I? I had lost myself in him, so totally, that walking away from him would be as effective as walking away from a part of myself.

And now, there was a part of him that would never leave me.

I imagine him in the hospital with Ava, waiting for her to wake, talking to her, telling her how sorry he was, maybe holding her hand, comforting her. From the small part of his conversation with the doctor I'd paid attention to, I knew he must have taken over her care. It was right that he had. It was the least he could do. Yet, that small gesture, combined with the way he'd fallen apart when he'd learned of the attack… it makes me sad, and that scares me. The fact that even though a woman is hurt, my most overwhelming emotion is jealousy and suspicion that she still held a part of Landon's heart.

I climb into bed and fall asleep almost immediately. I don't wake up until Landon slides in beside me, his skin cool from his shower. His arm encircles me, his chest a firm, hard wall against my back.

"Landon," I whisper his name, turning to face him.

"Shhh," he whispers, kissing me. His hand slides

down my naked body, heating my skin. I kiss him back, wanting him with a desperation that I can't explain.

His hands shake as he caresses me. He presses my body against his, as if he'll never let me go. "I love you," he whispers fiercely as he makes love to me. "I love you so much."

"I love you," I whisper back, holding him tight and praying that he somehow manages to exorcise the ghosts torturing him.

The next morning, he leaves the suite early, probably to go back to the hospital. I have a grapefruit for breakfast before I switch on the TV. Ava Sinclair's stabbing is a big part of the local news. The attack on the glamorous, thrice-divorced socialite by her unstable brother, and the billionaire ex-lover and owner of the hotel where the attack took place who came immediately to the rescue; it's like a soap opera, one I don't find particularly entertaining.

I put off the TV, not willing to watch anymore. I call Claude Devin and ask for Jules McDaniel's phone number. He gets it for me almost immediately. Jules sounds delighted to hear from me and invites me over.

Their house is a charming two story in a gated community. Cameron is at home, and Jules is obviously at the last stages of her pregnancy. We catch up and have lunch on the terrace before Cameron leaves for work. Neither of them bring up the case that's all over the news. It's as if they know how badly I want to escape it, and I'm infinitely grateful for that.

When I get back to the suite, Landon is alone. He's standing by the windows, drinking from a glass clinking with ice. I have time to look at him, and I see the utter exhaustion in his frame before he turns around and sees me.

His face relaxes into an expression that looks like relief. "I wondered where you were," he says, his voice soft.

From his face, I can see what he suspected, that maybe I'd left him again. "Claude could have told you. I went to see Jules."

"How is she?" he asks, his eyes softening.

"Ready to pop."

His lips lift in a small smile and he takes a step towards me. "I…" he looks down at his glass. "Would you like something to drink?"

I shake my head. "How is she?"

He knows I'm talking about Ava. "She's doing great. Evans is still missing, but many people are trying to find him. He wanted some more money, it seems, and when he found out she met with me in New York, it drove him crazy enough to hurt her."

I sigh, wishing the whole situation would somehow resolve itself as quickly as possible. "What will happen when they find him?"

Landon's face hardens. "He'll never hurt anyone again."

The conviction in his expression is hard to look at. I can't help thinking how he refused to do anything when Evans tried to hurt him, but obviously, with Ava, the rules are different. I swallow the lump in my throat. "When are we leaving?"

"As soon as you're ready."

The journey back to New York is another quiet one. Landon falls asleep almost immediately, probably from the stress. I find a book on my ereader and try to read, until I too, doze off.

At the apartment, we have an early dinner, still in silence. I have so much I want to say, but I don't know where to start. I don't even know if I want to say the things on my mind. When his nightmare wakes both of us a few hours later, I find myself wondering whom he's trying to save this time, Ava or me.

15

When distance grows between two people, sometimes it's almost palpable, in the silence, in the polite words, the total lack of real intimacy. I bury myself in my work, unable to find the words to tell Landon how I feel about Ava's attack and his reaction to it.

On his part, I know he's also working extra hard by how exhausted he is at night. How he falls asleep immediately after we make love, how he doesn't have the energy to get up during the night as he usually does, and his nightmares wake the both of us.

Three days after we returned from San Francisco, he

stops coming to bed at all, preferring to remain in his study all night. It's because of the nightmares, I tell myself, not because anything I feared would happen when he went to see Ava actually happened. Not because he can no longer bear to be with me when he'd rather be with her, comforting her, helping her get better.

The Friday morning, when he tells me over breakfast that he's planning to see a new therapist and has booked an appointment, I only nod silently. I feel almost as if he's a stranger, a stranger I love with my whole being, but a stranger nonetheless. I feel as if we're separated by a wall of silence, and I don't know if the words I have will break the walls or make them thicker.

Later that day, I leave work early for an appointment with my ob-gyn, who confirms that I'm pregnant. I no longer have any reason not to tell Landon. No reason, except the ghost of Ava Sinclair and her brother hanging over us like a permanent fixture in our lives.

When I get to the Swanson Court, there's a book launch and signing holding in one of the banquet halls, and a lot of fans and publishing industry types are coming and going through the lobby. After a short hesitation where I consider going to buy a book and getting it signed. I move on to the elevators, the possible long wait discouraging me.

The elevator opens almost as soon as I press the call button and I step inside, impatient to leave the crowded lobby. At the last moment, someone steps inside with me, and I look up just as the doors close to find myself staring at Evans Sinclair's malevolent face.

"Look normal, or I will shoot you. I promise."

I'm too shocked to do anything, even scream. Terror rises in my chest, choking me. His eyes roam from my face down to my feet and back up, almost black with hate. Everything that was once handsome about his face has disappeared, replaced by the sagging, blotched skin, and hollow look of an alcohol and substance abuser.

"Hi Rachel," he leers. He sounds almost good-natured, and that makes me even more afraid.

"What do you want?" I'm surprised that my voice isn't shaking, that I can still support myself on my own feet.

He chuckles. "Let me think… I want my hotel back. I want Landon Court to pay for taking it away from me. I want him to pay for using my sister."

"You stabbed your sister," I remind him.

"Shut up," he sneers. "Don't forget I have a gun, right here, under my jacket. I could shoot you and leave a nice surprise for your boyfriend."

From his face, I don't doubt that he would. If he has a gun. My eyes flick to the small camera at the top of the car. "Why should I believe that you have a gun?" I ask calmly.

He laughs again. "You want me to pull it out? Show you? So your security team will see it in the camera feed. "Good try, but I'm not dumb."

I breathe. "Then you know hurting me won't get you what you want? Neither will hurting Landon."

He shrugs. "I'm not going to get anything back anyway. I might as well hurt you."

The car stops and he gives me an expectant glance as the panel beeps for the keycard. "Go on," he says in a singsong voice. "Open the doors."

I retrieve the card from my purse and slide it into the panel. The doors slide open. Evans is watching me, and he motions with the hand inside his jacket pocket for me to walk inside ahead of him. I do as he wants, and once the doors slide closed behind me, he reaches for me, pulling me inside by my hair.

I fight him then, as soon as I see that the hand under his jacket is no longer holding the gun. I claw at him, my bag clattering to the floor as I attack him with all my strength. I use my nails, my teeth, and I scream, hoping that Esmeralda or one of the other staff is somewhere in the apartment.

He lands a punch on the side of my face, and I hit

the floor, almost passing out. I see two drops of blood from somewhere on my face stain the spotless white marble before there's another painful tug on my hair.

I start to scream again, until I feel the cold metal against my skin.

"I will shoot you," he whispers. "It'll be quicker than tossing you over the balcony. I'd like to see Landon Court try to fix you then, like he fixed the Gold Dust."

He starts to drag me by my hair again, and when he tosses me on the living room floor, I'm crying. It's not the physical pain that hurts the most. It's the fear and the regret. Regret that if he kills me, my child won't ever be born, that I'll never see Landon again. That the last memories he'll have of our relationship would be the growing distance, and the silence, not the love that fills me now when I think of him.

Evans is looking at my face and smiling. He squats down, close to me, and his grin widens. "You're ruining your mascara," he says, making an exaggerated sad face. Pulling a phone out of his pocket, he takes a picture. "Look at you," he says in that scary singsong voice. "Not so pretty now. Landon Court's girlfriend. I saw your pictures at the reopening of the Gold Dust. Did I tell you that your bastard boyfriend used to fuck my sister? That bitch. I think I'll rough you up a little bit more, send him a few pictures. What do you think?"

My head is beginning to pound where he hit me and

I can taste blood in my mouth. "You'll never get away with this," I manage.

He shrugs and binds my hands with duct tape, before moving to my feet. When he's done, he goes to the glass doors that lead to the balcony and slide them open.

The breeze that rushes inside the apartment is cold and biting. In desperation, I start to crawl, even though I know I probably won't get far. I'm going to die, I realize, tears beginning to flow again. My poor baby. Laurie, Dylan, my family… and Landon! Landon, who will never forgive himself. This will surely kill him.

"Where are you going?" I hear Evans ask cheerfully. He comes over and pulls me to my bound feet, then drags me out to the balcony. "Nice day isn't it?"

I look out at the city. It has always been beautiful to me from this height, but now it's just terrifying. Evans releases me and I brace my hands on the balustrade, dragging my feet as I try to put as much space between us as possible.

He looks at my efforts, his expression amused. Then he looks down at the traffic below. "Do you think it feels good, when you're falling?"

My cheeks are wet. I don't answer. I'm thinking of Landon. Please let there be a way for him to get through this.

"I'm talking to you." Evans prompts.

"I don't know," I whisper through my tears.

He smiles. "I don't know," he mimics, then adds under his breath. "Bitch."

I hear a sound from the living room, and I almost scream, but then Evans reaches for his gun, whipping it out and pointing in the direction of the sliding doors. The curtains are billowing and I'm too far away to see inside, but somehow, I know it's Landon in the apartment.

"Rachel?" I hear his voice, and even though it's the sweetest sound I've ever heard in my life, I'm still paralyzed by fear. Evans has the gun pointed at the door, and I know he won't hesitate to shoot."

"He has a gun!" I scream desperately. "He has a gun."

Evans ignores me, keeping the gun pointed at the curtains. A moment later, they part, and Landon is standing there. He looks at me, taking in my bound hands and feet. I see his jaw tighten as his eyes go to Evans.

"What do you want?" he asks.

"What do you think?"

Landon looks at me again then turns back to Evans. "You're not going to get it."

Evans smiles. "I think I already have."

"Really?" Landon sounds so calm, but I can see the vein in his jaw, working furiously. "You're a wanted man. You're going to jail. You won't get your hotel back, and you won't get away with whatever you plan to do here."

Evans is listening quietly. "You have no idea how much I hate you, how much I've hated you, all these years. I loved her, and she chose you, over and over again. Ava was perfect, and you ruined her. You made her give you all the time, the attention she should have given me."

Landon looks confused. "Your sister…"

"Yes…!" Evans screams. "I loved her, and you took her from me, and then you stole my hotel." He calms, very suddenly. "Maybe I won't get my hotel back, but then, maybe I don't want it anymore. Maybe I won't even get out of here, or get away with this…" he waves the gun around. "But I'm going to hurt you Landon Court. And you're never going to forget about me."

I still don't know exactly what happened next. All I remember is watching as Evans' gun arm started to turn toward me as if in slow motion. Then Landon, moving through the air like a projectile, launching himself at Evans. The huge roar as the gun went off, and my scream as they both started to go over the balustrade, then the thud as I hit the floor and everything went black.

16

The apartment has never felt so empty and silent. Everything has been professionally cleaned, the blood on the floor in the foyer, which, along with my scattered purse had first alerted Landon that something was wrong. The blood on the balcony is gone too, as well as the horror on the sidewalk.

I walk through the rooms, the silence bringing tears to my eyes.

Landon!

In his study, everything is off; the computers, the phone, no blinking lights to indicate that he's just taken a break and will soon be back to work.

On the desk, the picture I gave him still has pride of

place beside the computer screen. I look at my face, my attempt at a sultry expression, my body under the sheet… I'd been so happy then. And now…

Suddenly all the events of the evening of Evans attack rush into my head, and my eyes swell. I collapse on Landon's chair, surrounded by the smooth leather as sobs wrack my body.

Oh, Landon!

I'm still crying when I hear a noise at the open door. I look up to see Joe is standing at the doorway.

"Miss Foster?" He hasn't left the apartment since we returned from the hospital.

"Yes." I paste a smile on my face. "Yes?"

"The nurse. He's leaving."

I nod and get up. In the hall, Gerry, the short but muscular private nurse is waiting.

"Is he awake?" I ask.

Gerry shakes his head. "I changed the dressing on the wound and gave him something for the pain, so he'll be out all night. By tomorrow, I think he'll be able to get up and walk around."

I smile at him, watching as Joe leads him to the foyer. Just then, my phone rings.

"Hey," a soft voice says. It's Laurie. We've talked every day since the night of the attack, when she called while I was in the hospital, still in shock, and Landon was getting stitched up for the bullet that tore through his shoulder.

"Hey, Laurie," I reply softly. "How's it going?"

"Just checking on you. How is he?"

"Asleep." I swallow another set of tears. I'd been treated for my bruises and cuts, and I assured the doctors that everything else was fine, but I hadn't counted on the mental stress, the terror that never seemed to go away.

"How are you?"

"I'm fine," I say. It has become easier to tell people that, even though I only have to close my eyes to hear the sound of the gunshot, and see Landon going over the balcony.

"Are you sure?" She sounds worried. The last thing I want is for her to cut her honeymoon short because of me.

"We're both alive, Laurie. That's what matters."

When I end the call, Joe is standing at the entrance to the foyer.

"Thank you," I tell him, it's the first thing I've really said to him since that day. "Thanks for saving his life."

He is silent, and in his face, I see genuine emotion. "I should have been here earlier."

I shake my head. "No, you came right on time." Landon had pressed the emergency button on his phone as soon as he'd seen the blood in the foyer. So even while he was talking to Evans, trying to buy time, Joe had already been on his way.

I sigh, remembering the horror of watching as Landon charged Evans. I remember screaming and losing consciousness when I heard the gunshot. The bullet had slowed Landon down, just as the recoil made Evans unsteady on his feet. That was what sent Evans over the balustrade and made it possible for Joe to grab hold of Landon just before he went over.

Joe leaves me standing in front of the study, going back to his position in a corner of the living room. Sometimes, he joins Esmeralda in the kitchen when she comes up, but he's always here, within hearing distance, and there's something comforting about it.

I make my way upstairs. In the bedroom, the curtains are drawn, leaving the room dark and silent except for the sound of Landon's breathing as he sleeps. Going to stand beside the bed, I study his peaceful face. He is shirtless, his shoulder covered with white bandages, his hair ruffled, and his breaths slow and calm.

I sigh softly, my heart tightening as I stroke his hair. He had taken that bullet for me, because we'd both realized, as Evans turned the gun toward me, that he was going to shoot me, just to hurt Landon. That was why Landon had launched himself at him. That was why he'd risked his own life, knowing that he could get shot, or worse, go over the balcony.

I strip off my clothes, and when I'm wearing only my underwear, I join him in the bed, laying on my side so I can watch his beautiful face. "I love you," I whisper.

He doesn't reply, of course, but in the way his breathing changes, I feel as if he can hear me.

When I wake up, Landon is watching me. My eyes flutter open to find his blue gaze locked on my face and filled with emotion – love and intense relief.

I smile at him, leaning up on an elbow.

"You're awake."

"Yeah." He frowns. "I feel as if I've been asleep for weeks."

"A few days on and off, to give your shoulder time to heal," I search his face for any signs of pain. "How're you feeling?"

"Aching."

There's a fresh jug of water on a tray on the

nightstand. "Would you like some water?"

Landon nods slowly. "Yes," he says, then as I start to get up, he reaches out a hand to stop me. "But don't go yet." He sighs. "I just want to look at you."

My eyes fill with tears. "Landon…"

His breath hitches and he takes my hand in his, squeezing it as my eyes water again.

"You're shaking."

I smile through my glistening eyes. "I know."

His eyes close.

"Let me get you that water," I say.

"Wait." I watch his throat work as he swallows. "I'm sorry," he says. "I'm so sorry about Evans, for everything you went through… If only I'd listened to you after the thing with the car…" There are tears in his eyes.

"It doesn't matter," I whisper. "It's over now."

"It matters to me. I… God!" His throat works again. "When I saw you out there with him, I think a part of me died, of fear. I would die without you, Rachel. You are my life."

Now I'm crying. "I love you so much." My voice breaks, "When I saw you start to go over, I think my heart stopped beating."

"You think?" He gives me a teasing grin. "You

passed out."

I laugh through my tears. "Yeah, I did."

"When Joe pulled me back, and I saw you lying there, for a moment I thought I failed and that he hit you." He shakes his head. "Joe had to pry me off you."

"They sedated you because you kept on screaming about me." I smile. "They couldn't work on your wound."

He chuckles, and for a long moment, we lie there grinning at each other. Then I get up and fetch him the water. He drains the glass, then sighs and closes his eyes, resting his head back on the pillows.

"Do you want to go back to sleep?"

"No." His eyes open, and he taps my side of the bed. "Come back."

I do as he says, going back to lie beside him.

"The reason I was home early that day…" He stops and takes my hand again. "I wanted to talk to you, about San Francisco, about Ava, about the fact that I could see that I was losing you."

"You weren't…"

He shakes his head. "You were here, physically, but emotionally, you were drifting away. I could feel it, and I knew it had something to do with Ava, her stabbing, how I reacted to it..."

"It doesn't matter now," I tell him. "I love you, more than anything. I don't care about Ava now."

"But at the time?"

I sigh. "I was… I don't know what I was feeling. That she still meant too much to you. That was why you wouldn't get Evans locked up after he tried to hit you with his car, why you were so broken up when you heard about her stabbing… She told me, more than once, that you always came back to her, and that I was only temporary. She's known you far longer than I have, and she was so confident... I tried to ignore it, but watching you so devastated about her, it all came back."

He sighs. "She always came back, Rachel, after every divorce or high-profile breakup, and if I was single, which I was mostly, I let her in, because she already knew, more than anyone else, that I didn't want permanence, at least I didn't, before you."

I close my eyes. "She made me think she was the great love of your life."

"You're the great love of my life," he grins. "And I have a scar to prove it.

I smile sadly. "You're already joking about it. It's going to take a while for me."

Landon sighs and squeezes my hand. "About Ava..." he pauses. "We dated after college. I was working here, trying to do something with the hotel. She was attending college in the city, and I knew some of her extended family. We were set up, and we hit it off because, according to her, she didn't want anything permanent or exclusive. She said she didn't want love. Which was perfect for me, because I had no intention of giving it and ending up like either of my parents.

"What happened?"

"She used to leave, come back, and then leave again. I didn't understand it then. I thought it was fine that she wasn't committed because it meant that I wouldn't hurt her when I decided to walk away. I didn't realize until recently that she was trying…"

"To make you admit that you loved her."

Landon nods. "She wanted me to realize that I couldn't do without her. Every time she abandoned me to go to Capri with some fashionable trust-fund baby, or some software billionaire, she was asking me to come after her, and every time I didn't, she became more frustrated. She finally proposed, some leap year thing… and I said no. A week later she was married to a European racecar driver."

"She thinks she broke your heart," I say.

"She told you that. Trust me, she knows it isn't true. When she left her husband a few years later, she asked me if I hadn't been able to love her because I'd been too busy working to restore the Swanson Court Hotels. I told her the truth. I had no intention of ever making that kind of commitment," he looks at me. "At the time."

I imagine how Ava must have felt. "Yet you got together again."

Landon sighs. "I thought she understood that we were just people who knew each other very well. I never stood in the way of her relationships. I never wanted to. After her last divorce, she showed up but I let her know I was no longer interested."

"That was before we met."

He nods. "I've thought of her only as an old friend for a few years now."

"She made me feel like I was just someone temporary in your life, and she was much more than that to you." I sigh. "When she was hurt and you were so shaken… I was jealous and scared…and ashamed of my reaction. She was fighting for her life and all I could think about was losing you."

"You're never losing me, Rachel." His eyes linger on my face. "As for Ava, at the hospital, she said some things that made it clear that I had to let her know, very plainly, that we would never be more than friends again." He's still holding my hand, caressing my fingers with his. "You own me Rachel, every part of me. Knowing you're mine is what keeps me going. It's what makes it all meaningful. Before I met you, I thought I liked being alone. I took pride in not needing anyone. But I need you, and I'd give up everything just for you to never doubt that again."

"You don't have to give up anything," I reply softly. "I love you. Helplessly and completely, Landon."

He smiles, then his eyes close. "I'm exhausted," he says, still smiling. "Who knew intense declarations of love could be this tiring?"

I chuckle, then remember the one thing I still haven't told him. "I need to tell you something," I whisper, suddenly anxious.

He opens his eyes again, a worried frown creeping into his face. "What is it?"

I take a deep breath. "I'm… I'm pregnant."

He doesn't reply at first, the small frown still in place on his face. Will he hate me for not telling him sooner? I swallow and continue, "I found out in Barbados, and I wanted to tell you, but when I called... I trail off. "Well, you know what happened when I called."

His eyes close again, but not before I see the hurt clouding their blue depths. I quickly continue. "When

Evans...” I stop and close my eyes. “I couldn’t stop thinking about how I didn’t tell you, how I’d never get a chance to.”

“Stop…” His chest rises. “I understand how you felt, I do.” He sighs. “You know now that everything I do, work, solving the problems that have come up in the last few weeks, is so that I can get them out of the way and come home to you. Meeting with Ava, trying to find Evans, it was always about making sure he could never hurt you, because I’d rather die than let anyone hurt you.”

Tears sting at my eyes. “I know.”

“I hate that you felt unsure of me, and I take the blame for that. You’ll never have cause to doubt me again,” he says. “I promise. Everything I am, everything you want, I’ll give you, and if you let me, I’ll give everything I have, for you, for us, and for our child.”

I smile through my tears. “I only want you,” I whisper.

“All of me,” he says softly. “You already have all of me.”

Epilogue

The dinner is Landon's idea. Two weekends after Laurie and Brett return from their honeymoon. It's also my birthday. He reserves one of the restaurants in the Swanson Court Hotel and invites my whole family.

"You're glowing," is the first thing my mother whispers to me. She looks pleased. I haven't told her yet about the baby, but I will, soon. For now, it's something precious, just between Landon and me.

"Laurie is the one who's glowing like a lightbulb," I reply. It's true. Brett and Laurie can hardly keep their hands off each other. They keep whispering to each other and laughing at private jokes.

"Well, Happy Birthday," Mom says. She has already told me that, earlier on the phone. "My little baby all grown up!" She's smiling, her eyes bright.

My eyes water and I embrace her, wondering if I'm feeling emotional because I'm pregnant, or because I'm so happy.

My dad looks sad when he comes to put his arms around me. "Children grow up too fast," is all he says, kissing the top of my head.

Dylan is here with Kelly, his girlfriend, who finally said yes to dating him. She's very quick to laugh, and Dylan, my video-game loving brother, can hardly take his eyes off her. The Hayes are here, and Aidan too, with Elizabeth. Their play has continued to be a spectacular success, and every day the rumors in the art columns gain more conviction. They haven't announced any relationship, but seeing the two of them together, it's hard to imagine that they're not in love.

The gifts pile up on one of the tables. Thoughtful things I'm sure, acquired with me in mind, by the people who love me most in the world, and Landon, who loves me the way every girl should be loved by the man she has given her heart to.

He is devastating to look at in classic black tie, with his hair slicked back, his face free of any pressure, and suffused with happiness. He laughs with my father and uncle, teases his brother, tells my brother how lovely his girlfriend is, making both the girl in question and Dylan blush. Whenever he leaves my side, he returns in only a few minutes, his hand coming around my waist, his eyes caressing me with something that's love, and yet so much more.

There is a band with two singers, male and female. They take turns belting out mellow love songs while we all catch up, and everyone gets their chance to fuss over Landon again. When it's time to eat, the waiters set up a buffet. The informality is charming. Aidan and Elizabeth are the first to start dancing. The singers start a fast show tune, and they do a lively tap-dance that leaves us all clapping.

I see the look Landon exchanges with my dad, but I don't think much of it. When he signals the singers and they start playing one of my favorite love songs, I still don't get it. Landon takes my hand.

"Will you dance with me?" he asks.

"Of course." I follow him, to the floor, wondering as we start to dance, why no one joins us. He pulls me close and sways to the music, with everyone watching. I lean my head on his shoulder and let the music wash over me. The music, and my happiness.

As the last words fade away, Landon pulls away from me, and that's when I get it. For a second, my heart actually stops beating. I watch him drop slowly to one knee. On one level, I can hear the music, getting lower, mellower. I hear a sigh, maybe from my mom, a gasp too. Yet, I'm hardly conscious of anything, but Landon, in front of me, pulling a box out of his pocket, and opening it, offering me the dazzling ring inside.

"You know," he says softly. "You know everything."

I nod slowly.

"Will you marry me?"

I close my eyes, somewhere between ecstasy and hysteria and tears. "Yes," I whisper, as he gets up and catches me in his arms. "Yes, I will."

Seven Years Later

"I don't want to go to Windbreakers, I want to stay and see Uncle Aidan's new play."

"It'll probably still be showing in ten years when you're sixteen, maybe they'll let you in then."

Preston frowns. He's the spitting image of Landon, especially when he puts on his serious face. He peers into the stroller where his baby sister Penelope is sucking silently on her pacifier, blue eyes wide. "Then Penelope would be ten," he observes.

"An I'll be fhirtheen," Damien says with a sweet grin. He's the sweetest of my children, with the temperament of an angel and a smile to match.

I spy the car through the glass doors of the hotel. "Okay, let's go. Uncle Joe is waiting in the car."

"Uncle Joe!" Preston and Damien set off running. I think of telling them to slow down, but I decide not to bother. Outside, Joe is opening the door of the SUV, ready to make sure they don't go running off down the street, which I wouldn't put past them.

My phone rings.

"Hey, Laurie."

"Hey," I hear the smile in her voice. "Big party tomorrow, right?"

"Yeah," I laugh. It's my birthday, and there's going to be a party at our home upstate. "I've never felt so old."

"You've never been this old," she replies laughing.

"It has rewards," I say with a shrug, watching my boys through the glass, as they look up at Joe, probably peppering him with questions, or in Preston's case, asking about Joe's daughter Lindsay. She moved to New York to be closer to her father, and Preston has a big crush on her."

"Yes, it does." Laurie lowers her voice. "Sometimes, I don't believe that I'm a partner. I keep seeing myself as that junior associate cramming for the bar exam."

"I know what you mean." I'm a senior editor at Gilt Review now, and I still can't get used to the idea that I'm a boss of many.

Laurie sighs. "Call me when you get to the house. Brett and I will probably come in tonight and sic these mischievous kids on Mrs. Hayes. I plan to enjoy my weekend."

"Me too," I reply, laughing. Mrs. Hayes loves being surrounded by the kids, however, and she'll gladly take Laurie's kids and mine off our hands, giving me a break I really need, especially for my birthday. Between my work, the social events due to my position at Gilt, as Landon's wife, as well as my own life, the chance to kick back and just relax is invaluable.

I step through the glass doors in time to see Preston dodging Joe's arms and running down the sidewalk.

"I'll call you back," I tell Laurie, wondering how to run after my son while pushing a baby stroller.

"Daddy!" This time it's Damien, "Daddy," he cries louder, running in the same direction as his brother, as fast as his three-year-old legs can carry him.

Landon is stepping out of the car parked behind our SUV. He looks a bit travel weary, but aside from that little detail, in his tailored gray suit, and with his beautiful face, he's still every bit as devastating as he was the first day I saw him.

He keeps the traveling to a minimum because he can't stand to be separated from our children for any length of time, and also because we can't stand to be away from each other.

This time, it's a Swanson Court in Hong Kong, and it's almost ready for the grand opening. We all went with him, last weekend, and I came back a few days later with the children, leaving him to finalize plans for the opening while I went back to work. I missed him every second, but I knew without a doubt that his heart was always with me.

Landon lifts the boys in his arms, kisses both their foreheads and then smiles at me over their heads, starting to walk toward me.

"We were expecting you tomorrow," I whisper when he reaches me."

"I couldn't stay away a moment longer."

I smile. He smiles back, and I know we're just standing, smiling stupidly into each other's faces, but I don't care.

"Put me down, Dad," Preston complains finally, breaking the moment.

Landon chuckles and lowers the boys to the ground, then squats to look at Penelope in the stroller. She flutters her eyelashes at him, and he literally melts, the way he always does when she uses her considerable charms on him.

He looks up at me. In the background, I can hear Preston telling Joe that he wants to sit in front.

"I love you," Landon mouths the words silently.

I start to smile again. "I love you too."

The End

Author's Note

Thank you so much for reading Lost In You. I hope you enjoyed reading the books in this series. I loved writing about Landon and Rachel, and I'm going to miss them very much.

For those of you asking if Aidan Court will get a story, he definitely will. I'll start writing his story as soon as I finish a few other awesome books I'm already working on.

Thank you all so much for taking a chance on my books. What I enjoy is what some people might term as 'moderate success,' but it's more than I ever hoped or imagined and I'm immensely grateful for it. Thank you, my wonderful, awesome, beautiful readers, because of you, I can keep writing.

I don't have a Facebook group yet, but you can come over to my Facebook page and drop a note. I love to chat about my books.

I also love reviews! They keep me alive. Please review my books on Goodreads, and on as many purchase sites as you like. Use the recommend feature on Goodreads to share the word about my books to your friends and I'll be forever grateful.

If you want to get an email when the next book comes out, subscribe to my mailing list at www.serenagrey.com/alerts.

Connect with Serena

Facebook: www.facebook.com/authorserenagrey

Twitter: @s_greyauthor

Goodreads: www.goodreads.com/serenagrey

Author Website: www.serenagrey.com

Books by Serena Grey

A Dangerous Man Series

Awakening: A Dangerous Man #1

Rebellion: A Dangerous Man #2

Claim: A Dangerous Man #3

Surrender: A Dangerous Man #4

Undeniable

Swanson Court Series

Drawn to You

The Hooker

Addicted to You

Lost in You

Find at www.serenagrey.com/books

Made in the USA
Columbia, SC
28 February 2019